INSPECT

by Da...

The Seattle Repertory Theatre
Resident Company

SAMUEL FRENCH, INC.
45 WEST 25TH STREET   NEW YORK 10010
7623 SUNSET BOULEVARD HOLLYWOOD 90046
LONDON   TORONTO

ISBN 0 573 69368 4   Printed in U.S.A.

IMPORTANT BILLING AND CREDIT REQUIREMENTS

All producers of INSPECTING CAROL *must* give credit to the Author of the Play in all programs distributed in connection with performances of the Play and in all instances in which the title of the Play appears for purposes of advertising, publicizing or otherwise exploiting the Play and/or a production. The name of the Author *must* also appear on a separate line, on which no other name appears, immediately following the title, and *must* appear in size of type not less than fifty percent the size of the title type.

Produced at the Seattle Repertory Theatre on December 11, 1991, with the following cast:

M.J. (Mary Jane) McMann..... Barbara Dirickson
Wayne Wellacre................ R. Hamilton Wright
Zorah Bloch .... Marianne Owen
Luther Beatty.....................Danny Speigelman
Dorothy Tree-Hapgood ....Jeannie Carson
Sidney Carlton ....William Biff McGuire
Phil Hewlit .... Ethan Phillips
Walter E. Parsons ....Mark Smaltz
Kevin Emery .... Larry Paulsen
Bart Frances.............................Alban Dennls
Larry Vauxhall ....John Aylward
Betty Andrews ....Mary Anne Selbert

Director: Daniel Sullivan
Scenic Designer: Andrew Wood Boughton
Costume Designer: Robert Wojewodski
Lighting Designer: Rick Paulsen
Composer: Norman Durkee
Sound Designer: Michael Holten

CHARACTERS

Zorah Bloch—Founding director of The Soapbox Playhouse. In her 40's. Extremely self-concerned.

Sidney Carlton—In his 60's. A founding member of the Company. Kind but somewhat addled.

Dorothy Tree Hapgood—His wife. In her 60's. English and unable to lose her accent. A founding member.

Larry Vauxhall—In his 40's. Tough, intellectually vain Child of the '60's, still looking for a turn-on. A founding member.

Phil Hewlitt—In his 40'8. Small, obsessive usually plays the ineffectual character in any Soapbox production. A founding member.

Walter E. Parsons—African-American in his 30's. Recently taken up acting again after a stint in the armed forces. Good natured, excitable.

Luther Beatty—A large eleven-year-old. He's been playing Tiny Tim two years too long. Extremely friendly.

Kevin Emery—A nervous man in the impossible position of managing director. In his 40's. Afraid of Zorah.

M.J. (Mary Jane) McMann—In her 40's. A realist. She long ago realized that the Company hit bottom. She looks on now as a bemused observer. Founding member.

Betty Andrews—In her 40's. An inspector for the National Endowment for the Arts. A forbiding appearance. Bright red hair.

Bart Frances—A pleasant youth. Dresses in a motorcycle jacket and torn jeans.

Wayne Wellacre—In his 30's, in search of a new career in acting, no training, less talent, affable, eager to please.

SETTING: A mid-sized city in the Midwest.

ACT I

The stage and a portion of the auditorium of a mid-western regional theatre. The stage is thrust-style and is presently occupied by a unit set suggesting Dickens' London. M.J., the Stage manager, is preparing her table for the day's rehearsal. SHE sings to herself.

(WAYNE enters, nervously. HE carries a laptop word processor.)

WAYNE. Good morning. Hi. Am I too late?

M.J. Can I help you?

WAYNE. Is this the Soapbox Playhouse?

M.J. Yes.

WAYNE. I had an audition but I think I must be late.

M.J. With Zorah?

WAYNE. I don't know. (*Takes out brochure.*) Oh, yeah. Yeah With Zorah Bloch.

M.J. We're rehearsing now.

WAYNE. Yeah. I knew I was late.

M.J. I didn't know she had an appointment.

WAYNE. Well, it wasn't confirmed. I sent a postcard that I was going to be here. But ...

M.J. I don't think it's on her schedule.

WAYNE. I'm only here for the day so I was hoping she could work me in.

M.J. We're rehearsing now. We're just on a short break.

WAYNE. Oh, thanks. That's great. Are you an actress?

M.J. Only during periods of extreme necessity.

WAYNE. (*HE's on stage now.*) 'Cause I could see you've got on your costume.

M.J. Well actually these are my clothes. But you're right. I have been pressed into the service of this epic. I play the female population of London.

WAYNE. (*Impressed.*) Oh.

M.J. But mostly I'm the stage manager. You're going to have to clear off now.

WAYNE. I'll get right down. I just wanted to see how it feels.

M.J. Uh-huh. How's it feel?

WAYNE. Great. Big. But great.

M.J. This is big?

WAYNE. Bigger than my apartment.

M.J. Listen, this is a bad time ...

WAYNE. (*HE turns his back to the auditorium, then quickly wheels around, hump-backed, imitating the limp and withered hand of Richard the Third.*)
"Now is the winter of our discontent
Made glorious summer by this sun of York."

(*HE stops, savouring it.*)

M.J. You know this is a professional company.

WAYNE. I'm a professional. Or I was. I'd gotten about as far as I could go in data processing. I was good. I just wasn't feeling very fulfilled. So I'm following my bliss now.

M.J. (*HE's in the way.*) You'll have to clear off now.

WAYNE. (*Following her.*) You know Joseph Campbell? He's the guy who thought up *Star Wars*? You know, the movie?

M.J. Yeah.

WAYNE. Well, he didn't actually think it up, but he was a big influence on the people who did. Anyway, I was taking this potentiality seminar and we read this Joseph Campbell book about creation myths?

M.J. Yeah.

WAYNE. How there's all these ancient stories locked away inside us that can tell us how to lead our lives.

M.J. Oh?

WAYNE. So you just have to sort of "follow your bliss." It's kind of like "use the force" only not so violent. Anyway, that's what I'm doing. I'm following my bliss. (*Holding up his P.C.*) And I'm keeping a record of my experiences on the path.

M.J. Ok. But you have to be a union member to work here.

WAYNE. A union ... Oh. I get you. I get you. You have to be a union ... Oh God, why don't they *ever* give you a warning? Why don't they give you some kind of a ... you know, warning. There should be some kind of a warning. In the brochure here.

M.J. I think maybe you're just supposed to know that.

WAYNE. So what do I do now? I'm only in town for the day.

M.J. Hardly enough time to become professional.

WAYNE. Yeah. Well ... thanks. I appreciate your help.

WAYNE. (*Jumping up on stage.*) "Hey, lady. I like the way you move. I just had to tell you that. My engine's been kickin' over hard ever since I laid eyes on you."

M.J. Beg pardon?

WAYNE. That's from *Tijuana Truck Stop* by Terry Allen Anthony. That's my contemporary audition. You need two.

M.J. I know.

WAYNE. For contrast.

M.J. Yeah. Bye now.

WAYNE. (*As HE goes.*) Is there another theatre in town?

M.J. There's the lesbian theatre over at the Methodist Center.

WAYNE. Oh ... Do they ever use men?

M.J. You mean ...

WAYNE. On stage?

M.J. You'd have to ask.

(*ZORAH enters with LUTHER, a heavy set 10-year-old.*)

WAYNE. Ok. Thanks.

ZORAH. (*To Wayne.*) For Christ sakes, it's about time! The computer is *upstairs*. And as far as I'm concerned you can take the stupid thing back.

M.J. (*Hustling WAYNE out.*) No, this is not the computer guy. Mistaken identity.

WAYNE. Miss Bloch?

M.J. We're starting now.

(*M.J. shows WAYNE the door. HE exits.*)

ZORAH. Who was that?

M.J. I think I just saved you from a very painful experience.

ZORAH. Slightly creepy guy.

M.J. You don't know the half of it. Luther, you should be getting ready.

LUTHER. I don't come on for four more scenes.

ZORAH. Where were we?

M.J. The knocker.

ZORAH. The knocker. That's as far as we've gotten?

M.J. Yeah. (*Offering Zorah a jar of chocolate kisses from her desk.*) Have a kiss.

ZORAH. Get those out of here.

M.J. Can't. The actors expect it. Sort of my own little theatre tradition.

ZORAH. How can you eat those and stay so thin?

M.J. This is *all* I eat.

LUTHER. Wow. You must be a complete grease bag by now. (*Puts his hand in kisses' jar.*)

M.J. You want a ride home tonight? Keep it up.

LUTHER. Just one?

M.J. No.

ZORAH. Luther dear, your mother would be very angry with us if she thought you were eating candy at rehearsals.

LUTHER. But it's traditional.

M.J. Backstage. Now.

LUTHER. (*Going.*) We're nowhere near my scene.

ZORAH. (*To M.J.*) Why are we moving so slowly?

M.J. Well ...

ZORAH. (*With exaggerated concern.*) It's not like we have to stop to figure anything out. What's the difference this year?

M.J. Hmm. Let me see. Could it be Larry?

ZORAH. All right, no need for your withering irony.

M.J. Was I being ironic? I'm so ashamed.

ZORAH. Did I have another choice?

M.J. I'm not being critical.

ZORAH. I waited until the last possible minute before I asked him.

M.J. You want to know what's taking up time. I'm telling you.

ZORAH. No one else would do it. I couldn't *give* the role away. I'd have to put *you* on.

M.J. Why, you don't think our loyal subscribers would buy me as Scrooge?

ZORAH. After all these years they probably wouldn't even notice.

M.J. You ready to start?

ZORAH. At least you'd be easier to work with.

M.J. (*Ironically.*) Hey. Come on. Larry's a lamb compared to what he did last time.

ZORAH. Oh, now, let's not get into that ...

M.J. You have no idea how bad that was. You were sitting safe at home. We were the ones who had to make it through the performance.

ZORAH. I fired him, didn't I?

M.J. Yes, and you have just rehired him.

ZORAH. He's apologized for that.

M.J. Apologized? He spoke Spanish, Zorah. He performed the entire role of Scrooge in Spanish.

ZORAH. Shh-hh-hh!

M.J. Why did he do that? It was insane and it took four hours because nobody knew when to come in with their lines. What was that all about?

.ZORAH. He said he was protesting American involvement in Central America.

M.J. Oh for Christ's sake. Are we still involved?

ZORAH. I think so.

M.J. Oh, shit.

ZORAH. Larry's fine now. The divorce sort of took the edge off him, thank God.

M.J. That's not all Marci took off him.

(*The door to the lobby opens. DOROTHY enters with SIDNEY. DOROTHY is limping badly. SHE has a home-made splint on her foot, covered by a man's sweat sock. SIDNEY carries a donut-shaped pillow.*)

SIDNEY. (*To Dorothy.*) Careful, there're steps here.

DOROTHY. Of course there're steps here.

ZORAH. Dorothy?

DOROTHY. He tells me there are steps here.

M.J. What happened?

DOROTHY. Sorry. It's nothing. It's ridiculous.

SIDNEY. She won't see a doctor.

DOROTHY. Have we started?

ZORAH. Are you all right?

DOROTHY. It's nothing. Don't worry. The skirts will cover it.

ZORAH. What happened?

SIDNEY. Freezer accident.

M.J. What?

SIDNEY. Freezer accident. She—

DOROTHY. I open the freezer door and a sausage roll comes crashing down on my foot.

SIDNEY. My fault. I had my suppositories in there. (*HE produces a box of suppositories.*)

DOROTHY. He crams the thing with suppositories.

SIDNEY. There was a sale.

DOROTHY. Drives me up the pole.

M.J. You don't come on for a while. We're at the knocker.

SIDNEY. That's me. (*As HE exits, HE places his suppositories on M.J.'s table.*)

DOROTHY. (*To Sidney.*) Could you bring me a cup of coffee? (*To Zorah.*) I need to give a listen to this anyway. I think the accents have gone off. (*As DOROTHY sits, M.J. helps place her foot on the adjoining seat.*)

(*PHIL, a middle-aged actor, carries Luther on his shoulders. PHIL is having difficulty getting through a doorway.*)

PHIL. Zorah ... Zorah ...

M.J. We're not ready for you yet, Phil.

PHIL. I can't even get through the door with him.

ZORAH. He ducks. He always ducks.

PHIL. I'll have to come through on my knees. Is this the same door as last year?

ZORAH. Of course. Get down, Luther. Somebody help Luther down.

PHIL. Help *Luther*?

LUTHER. Here. I can do it. (*HE pulls himself up on the door frame and lowers himself to the floor.*)

ZORAH. I don't know how solid that is, Luther.

LUTHER. No problem.

ZORAH. Strong, huh? You put on a little muscle last summer, didn't you, you little pipsqueak?

LUTHER. Yeah.

ZORAH. You're going to be too big for this role next year.

LUTHER. Really?

M.J. (*Protecting Luther.*) We don't want to talk about next year now, do we?

PHIL. Zorah?

ZORAH. Yes, Phil.

PHIL. I was just talking to Larry—

M.J. Oh, shit.

PHIL. ... and we were thinking maybe we could find some other way for me to get Tiny Tim around? I can do it. I can lift him. I just wonder if it doesn't look funny.

ZORAH. What? That you're ...

PHIL. Yes ...

ZORAH. ... carrying him around?

PHIL. Yes.

PHIL. I know it's a a strong image and everything, but why should Cratchit be coddling him? I mean, if the kid's got this big and he's still using a crutch, maybe it's because I've been carrying him.

ZORAH. So then you *make* him walk.

PHIL. Yes. Yes. To make him strong.

ZORAH. (*At a loss.*) Uh-huh.

LUTHER. Yeah, watch. (*Leaping about on his crutch.*) Look out, dudes. I could beat you home so fast!

M.J. (*Restraining Luther.*) That's enough now, Luther. You're going to hurt yourself. Luther. Stop it!

PHIL. Well, that may be going a little too far, but you get the idea.

LUTHER. Wheelies!

M.J. (*To Zorah.*) Could we just say no to this idea and move on?

ZORAH. Phil, no. Thank you, Luther!

LUTHER. Cool.

PHIL. I may not be able to carry him anyway. My back is very weak. I've got this traveling pain in my right leg. Along the sciatic nerve.

M.J. Doesn't the sciatic nerve go down your other leg?

PHIL. I'm telling you ... It travels.

M.J. (*To Luther.*) Come on, Dude.

PHIL. (*Muttering to Dorothy.*) He is supposed to be Tiny. That's his name.

M.J. Come on, Phil. We're starting.

PHIL. (*To Zorah, privately.*) So I'm just an actor to you again? Someone you say "no" to?

ZORAH. (*Under her breath.*) Please, Phil.

PHIL. I'm feeling a little used.

ZORAH. This isn't the place for this.

PHIL. So where then?

ZORAH. Look, Phil, you must understand—we made a mistake.

PHIL. I didn't make a ...

ZORAH. All right, *I* made a mistake.

(*DOROTHY pores over a tattered manuscript.*)

PHIL. Are you saying it's over?

ZORAH. Phil, please, it never began. We slept together once. Sorry, Dorothy.

DOROTHY. No bother.

ZORAH. It was a mistake.

PHIL. It may have meant nothing to you, but I don't give myself away so freely.

ZORAH. You gave yourself away?

PHIL. Why then? Why'd you do it. Why'd you sleep with me?

ZORAH. I was drunk. You were begging me. I don't mean to diminish you, Phil. I'm sure you had a powerful experience. You're fixated. Understandably.

PHIL. And you're hiding. I know you're hiding.

ZORAH. I can't do this, Phil.

PHIL. Because you were fantastic. That was no mistake.

M.J. (*Entering.*) Zorah, can I talk to you?

ZORAH. Please.

PHIL. Overwhelming, I think, is the word.

M.J. (*Crosses to Zorah.*) Excuse me, Phil, am I interrupting something?

PHIL. (*As HE goes.*) Something? I believe it's something. Yes, I do. (*To Zorah.*) And I believe it meant something to others, too.

M.J. (*To Zorah.*) We are rapidly eating up the four days of rehearsal time you allow yourself for this project.

ZORAH. They've been doing it every December for twelve years. You think they don't remember how it ends?

M.J. Walter's never done it.

ZORAH. Oh, yes, Walter.

M.J. You want him to go on cold?

ZORAH. It's your job to push me.

M.J. That's what I'm doing.

(*WALTER enters in the hooded costume of the Ghost of Christmas Yet-To-Come. HE carries a bony, wooden hand.*)

WALTER. Hey ...

LUTHER. Whoa! Sca-a-*ry*!

WALTER. (*Referring to his costume.*) This thing is very funky.

M.J. Walter, you're in the wrong ghost.

ZORAH. Hi, Walter!

M.J. That's the last ghost.

WALTER. I don't think this one got cleaned.

M.J. You'll only have it on for five minutes.

WALTER. Let me do it without the hood. You wouldn't last thirty seconds in here.

M.J. (*To Walter.*) You can't do it without the hood, Walter. They'd recognize you from earlier in the play.

WALTER. (*To Zorah.*) Why is recognizing me necessarily so bad?

ZORAH. Welcome, Walter. Welcome to the Soapbox Playhouse. Oh, good, good. They lengthened it.

WALTER. Yeah. Listen ...

ZORAH. Would you like a little kiss?

WALTER. Pardon me?

(*SHE offers a chocolate kiss.*)

WALTER. Oh. I get you. No. No. I was just—

ZORAH. We're all very excited to have you in the company, Walter. You probably know that by now.

WALTER. Thanks ...

ZORAH. It's no secret I ruffled a few feathers when I started this multi-cultural initiative. I don't have to tell you this company was pretty white. (*Confidentially.*) *All* white. Let's be frank. But here you are.

WALTER. Yep.

ZORAH. And here you are in The World of Charles Dickens.

WALTER. Yep.

ZORAH. This is non-traditional casting. And you are breaking new ground for us.

WALTER. I'm very proud. Do I have to wear this hood?

(Sound of CHAINS offstage)

ZORAH. Well ... I think ....

(SIDNEY, dressed as Marley's Ghost, enters, carrying a cup of coffee. His CHAINS drag the ground noisily.)

M.J. Sidney! The chains!

(SIDNEY stops.)

M.J. We're trying to work something out.

(SIDNEY stands still and sips his coffee.)

ZORAH. *(To Walter.)* You have to wear the hood. The Ghost of Christmas Yet-To-Come is featureless. He's anonymous.

WALTER. *(Confidentially.)* I don't think this was cleaned.

ZORAH. *(Looking his costume over.)* It looks fine.

WALTER. No. Zorah, it has a very rancid smell. Something must have crawled up in here and died.

(ZORAH looks at him.)

WALTER. Who was in this thing?

ZORAH. It was ...

WALTER. Seriously.

M.J. Walter ...

WALTER. Seriously. I just need to be able to breathe.

(*ZORAH exits quickly, overcome.*)

SIDNEY. Oh, dear ...

WALTER. What'd I say?

M.J. My fault. I should have told you.

WALTER. What?

SIDNEY. It was Sherman's.

M.J. Sherman was her husband. It was his costume.

DOROTHY. Yes. He died last year.

WALTER. Oh, shit.

M.J. She's just freaked out from the smell thing.

WALTER. So I'm playing the ghost of her dead husband?

M.J. (*Winking broadly.*) Or maybe Husbands Yet-To-Come.

WALTER. Let me ask you something: if I'm your first black actor, how come I have to walk around and point with this white hand? (*HE demonstrates as HE puts his hood up.*) What does this look like? Does this look multi-cultural to you?

M.J. This is the hand we use, Walter. What? You want us to paint it black? Ghosts are white, Walter. They're just ... white.

WALTER. Well now. That's amazing. After I die I can buy on credit.

M.J. Walter ... We don't have time to paint it black.

WALTER. I'll do it myself. (*HE exits.*)

SIDNEY. Can I move? Dorothy's coffee's getting cold.

M.J. Yes. But can you just pick up the chains?

DOROTHY. I'll take it.

M.J. (*Into intercom.*) Larry Vauxhall on stage, please. We're trying to begin the Knocker Scene. Larry Vauxhall.

(*As SIDNEY DOROTHY and LUTHER exit, KEVIN enters. HE is dressed in a business suit and is extremely agitated.*)

KEVIN. Is Zorah here? (*KEVIN takes a suppository from the box on M.J.'s table.*)

M.J. Kevin, we're rehearsing.

KEVIN. Honest, I just need her for one sec.

M.J. I'll get her. (*SHE exits.*)

SIDNEY. Kevin, you're about to eat one of my suppositories. (*HE exits.*)

KEVIN. Luther ... (*HE takes the bowl of candy and approaches Luther.*) I got the computer turned on.

LUTHER. Good.

(*LUTHER reaches for a candy. KEVIN covers the bowl with his hand.*)

KEVIN. I just need to know one little thing, and I can take it from there, ok?

LUTHER. Sure.

KEVIN. I was entering some information, and it just went blank.

LUTHER. It crashed.

KEVIN. Of course it crashed. But why?

LUTHER. Ok. You probably changed your option "Letter Quality Printer" from "N" to "Y." You just need to boot it up. Hit your Reset. It'll give you a soft boot.

KEVIN. Reset?

LUTHER. Yeah. It's that little button that says "Reset."

KEVIN. Oh, that. Yeah, of course.

LUTHER. But for now you should be doing a manual backup.

KEVIN. Let me run the business? (*HE tousles Luther's hair and offers candy bowl.*)

LUTHER. Cool. (*LUTHER takes a handful of candy and exits.*)

(*M.J. enters with ZORAH.*)

ZORAH. Looking for me?

KEVIN. (*After a pause.*) Actually I just came in to ask you not to leave the building at lunch if that's possible. If you could drop by my office, I need to discuss a couple of money things with you.

ZORAH. Money things?

KEVIN. (*Leaving, to M.J.*) Just don't let her get away before she talks to me.

M.J. Okay!

ZORAH. What are the things?

KEVIN. You've got a rehearsal.

ZORAH. Tell me.

KEVIN. Honestly. Not for now.

ZORAH. Kevin. I'm not rehearsing until you tell me. You've got a very stubborn Lithuanian here.

KEVIN. Sorry, Mary Jane.

(M.J. exits.)

KEVIN. I just want to go over the subscription figures with you. That's all.

ZORAH. What figures?

KEVIN. It's the ... a ... the subscription goal. We didn't reach our subscription goal.

ZORAH. We didn't?

KEVIN. No.

ZORAH. What was the goal?

KEVIN. Four thousand subscribers.

ZORAH. What did we get?

KEVIN. Two.

ZORAH. Two?

KEVIN. Two thousand.

ZORAH. I know what "two" means, Kevin. I didn't think we'd ended up with two subscribers. For God's sake, give me some credit.

KEVIN. Anyway—

ZORAH. Anyway we got half. That's the news?

KEVIN. Yeah. So. To make a long story short, we've got a cash-flow problem.

ZORAH. How bad?

KEVIN. We have no cash.

ZORAH. You mean we're broke.

KEVIN. Yes.

ZORAH. Oh my God.

KEVIN. Zorah ...

ZORAH. How did this happen? Oh my God!

KEVIN. Listen to me ...

ZORAH. I feel sick to my stomach.

KEVIN. I asked you to see me later.

ZORAH. You came down here ... you came all the way down here to tell me to talk to you later. And I'm supposed to say, "Oh, sure. Great, Kevin, money things. Talk to you later?"

KEVIN. I'm sorry.

ZORAH. Shit. Shit shit shit. I'm sorry. I'm Lithuanian. I have a lot of anger. It isn't your fault. I'm sorry. God! What happened?

KEVIN. Well the market's a little soft right now.

ZORAH. No, I mean what happened to my life? You're new here. You don't know who I was when I started this place. I wanted to change people. I wanted to erase the borders between theatre and life. I wanted to hold up the mirror.

KEVIN. Yeah. To nature?

ZORAH. Yes. What was I thinking? Change people? What did I mean, change people? Into what?

KEVIN. Non-subscribers, maybe. I'm sorry.

ZORAH. You can't change this audience. You can't do what you want. You have to do what *they* want. And now you tell me *they* don't even want what they want. Last season. God! Have you ever seen anything that boring?

KEVIN. I thought your production of *Harvey* was interesting.

ZORAH. I'll tell you. However much we complain about it, at times like this all I can say is: *Thank God* for the National Endowment for the Arts.

KEVIN. Yeah.

ZORAH. I know that's heresy. I know it's a pitiful little grant compared to what other companies get. But right now thirty thousand dollars is going to get us into next year.

KEVIN. That's the second thing I wanted to talk to you about.

ZORAH. What?

KEVIN. The grant.

ZORAH. Oh, Kevin, they didn't cut us back again?

KEVIN. Well ...

ZORAH. Oh, Kevin. This is just embarrassing.

KEVIN. Yeah.

ZORAH. Why do they *do* this? They cut us two thousand dollars last year. They just nip away at you, you know.

KEVIN. Yeah.

ZORAH. Take little chunks out of you. As if there was an adequate amount there to start with.

KEVIN. Yeah.

ZORAH. So what's the damage this year?

KEVIN. They aren't giving us anything. (*Pause.*) They've decided to withhold the grant in its entirety, pending an artistic evaluation. Apparently they have questions about what they call—uh—well. Here. It's here. (*Reads from letter.*) "...a significant artistic deficit" (*Pause.*) Word is we got a pretty bad report from last year's evaluator.

(*Pause.*)

ZORAH. That little shit.

KEVIN. Yes, well.

ZORAH. Mincing little snitch!

KEVIN. He loved the posters.

ZORAH. Pluralistic pederast.

KEVIN. Well, I don't know if you can ...

ZORAH. What do they want? They said we were too white, that we weren't hiring people who were ... what is it?

KEVIN. People of color.

ZORAH. And we did that. And we have done that. I've bent over backwards to be multi-cultural, Kevin, you agree.

KEVIN. You've tried.

ZORAH. I've tried? I hired Walter! They want us to balance our books. I hire you. Last year they're big on new works, I do that play about colon cancer, and that was not easy for me, Kevin, as you know, having lost Sherman just two days before the first rehearsal.

KEVIN. He didn't have colon ...

ZORAH. And now this. I've given them everything they've asked for, Kevin, and now they want, what? Quality? We never get a break, do we.

KEVIN. Well, that's the odd thing. We could still have a chance. They're sending out one last evaluator.

ZORAH. What'd you mean?

KEVIN. Well, apparently this is the way they do it. The N.E.A. keeps the money until they get his report. If the report is good, they let the money go.

ZORAH. To us.

KEVIN. Of course to us.

ZORAH. What if the report is bad? What happens to the money then?

KEVIN. (*Losing control.*) I don't know, Zorah! They give it to Robert Mapplethorpe's estate! How the hell should I know! We don't get it!

ZORAH. (*The victim.*) All right. That's what I was asking.

M.J. (*Entering.*) Could you two possibly keep it down?

KEVIN. We're finished, Mary Jane.

M.J. (*Shouting off.*) Let's get going, folks!

ZORAH. (*To Kevin.*) Who's coming this time? Is it the same guy as last year?

KEVIN. They don't say.

ZORAH. (*Takes the letter.*) Are you sure?

KEVIN. Whoever it is, he's due here sometime this week.

ZORAH. This week? He's going to see *this*!

KEVIN. Yeah.

M.J. Who's going to see this?

(*LARRY enters in the severe black coat and hat of Ebeneezer Scrooge. From the waist down, however, he is dressed in street clothes—worn-out jeans and Birkenstocks. He has PHIL in tow. The COMPANY enters and settles in the auditorium.*)

LARRY. Can we interrupt?

M.J. We're starting, Larry.

LARRY. Zorah, listen, we just had this great idea. Take a look at this. Come on, Phil. Let's ...

PHIL. I don't know about this.

LARRY. You're going to back out on me now?

PHIL. (*To Zorah.*) It's just kind of a green room joke.

LARRY. You thought this was a great idea.

PHIL. Come on, we were goofing. Let's not ...

LARRY. Are you going to do this with me or not?

M.J. Oh, can we please get started now, Larry? What are you doing?

LARRY. Zorah, this is just a thing for the ending. We wouldn't be rewriting. We wouldn't be tampering with your sacred text.

ZORAH. Welcome back, Larry.

(M.J. laughs)

LARRY. What. What does that mean. This is typical of me?

M.J. (*From across the room.*) We love ya', Larry.

LARRY. (*Still to Zorah.*) Because I look for new things?

(ZORAH is too upset to handle this.)

KEVIN. Look. Larry. You remember, don't you? You agreed, contractually, you'd come back and play Scrooge *as written*. Like you originally did it.

M.J. In English.

LARRY. We're talking about the art here now. I don't think this is your bailiwick. We have a history together. This is how we work. Why are you bringing that up again anyway, M.J.? I was bored. You have any idea what it's like to play these roles year after year? We get bored ... Comprende?

M.J. Watch it.

SIDNEY. We're not bored.

DOROTHY. Not at all.

LARRY. You get bored. You want to change things. This is not that. This is different.

KEVIN. And what is this?

LARRY. This isn't a rewrite. It's a cut. A tiny cut at the end.

KEVIN. Oh. Well. I don't know. If it's a cut. Zorah. He's only talking about a cut.

ZORAH. What's the cut, Larry?

LARRY. At the end.

ZORAH. Yes.

LARRY. When I get to the office before Cratchit to surprise him. Well. (*To Phil.*) Let's just do it.

(*PHIL begins to mime running in place.*)

LARRY. Bong. Bong. Bong. Bong. Bong. Bong. Bong. (*As Scrooge.*) "Late as usual." (*HE laughs, giddy with joy.*) "Here he comes. Here he comes."

(*PHIL rushes into office as Cratchit. HE warily eyes Scrooge as HE mimes taking off his hat and scarf.*)

SCROOGE. (*Suddenly stern.*) "You're late, Mr. Cratchit."

CRATCHIT. "Sorry, Mr. Scrooge. I am behind my time."

SCROOGE. "Indeed you are."

CRATCHIT. "It shan't be repeated. I'm afraid we were making rather merry yesterday."

SCROOGE. "This is the last straw, Cratchit."

CRATCHIT. "But, Mr. Scrooge, it's only once a year..."

SCROOGE. "I'm not going to stand for this anymore. You leave me no choice."

(SCROOGE puts his head down and goes back to work.
   CRATCHIT sits, tense and fearful.
A long moment.)

LARRY. Curtain. (*LARRY turns to Zorah.*) Reaction?

(There is none.)

PHIL. We were kidding around.
LARRY. (*Very excited.*) Yes, we were. And then it suddenly, Blamo! It just started to make so much sense!
KEVIN. What makes sense? That's the end of the play?
LARRY. Yes.
KEVIN. Scrooge doesn't say, "You leave me no choice but to *raise* your wages"?
LARRY. Correct.
ZORAH. That's not an ending, Larry. The play would have no ending.
LARRY. I think that's the point.
ZORAH. What? I'm sorry, I'm thick. I'm missing this.
LARRY. See, we're playing this against strong audience expectations. They're waiting for a line. But we don't give it to them. They are listening now. Blamo!
ZORAH. There is no resolution.
LARRY. Exactly. *There is no resolution:* We are headed for the goddamn millennium, you know. The goddamn 21st century. So we *know* there's no resolution. So let's just *say that.* I mean, come on, haven't you ever at least wondered how long Scrooge could keep all this "what a remarkable boy" shit going? I mean isn't that a question? And shouldn't we ask it?

ZORAH. I think the question we have to ask, Larry, is why did I agree to let you play this role again?

M.J. This isn't going to be constructive.

ZORAH. (*To Larry.*) Honestly it's not your fault. You're who you are. It's me. Why did I expect you would have changed?

LARRY. *I* haven't changed?

M.J. Could we have places please?

LARRY. Wait a minute. Wait a minute. *I* haven't changed?

KEVIN. Come on now, Larry.

LARRY. I want to show you something. (*Exiting.*) Thanks for exploring with me, Phil. (*HE goes.*)

M.J. Could we have places please.

KEVIN. I'm sorry, Zorah.

ZORAH. Of course you are, Kevin.

LARRY. (*Re-enters holding a prop papier mache turkey.*) *I* haven't changed? (*Indicating the turkey.*) Look at this. Twelve years ago, brand new, this was a thoroughly unconvincing piece of work ...

KEVIN. Larry ...

LARRY. No. No. You are as responsible for this as she is. Every year at this time, in *your* theatre, as some hideous practical joke, Scrooge sends the Cratchits a filthy cardboard turkey. Look. I want you to look at this. Someone has actually carved initials in this turkey.

SIDNEY. (*Seated in the audience.*) Works from out here, Larry. Looks like a turkey.

DOROTHY. (*From the audience.*) Don't hold it by the neck, dear.

KEVIN. Larry. Calm down. There's no problem here. We could throw the turkey out. We could get another turkey, M.J. ...

LARRY. *I* don't change. Look at this. (*Shaking a piece of scenery.*) Can you believe this thing is still standing? *I* don't change.

ZORAH. Why are you doing this?

KEVIN. Now, Zorah—

ZORAH. We have an opportunity to actually *make* money *once* a year. You're begrudging us that?

SIDNEY. The public needs this, Larry. They'd tear the place down if we didn't do this.

DOROTHY. It's a tradition, isn't it? Like trimming the tree and such.

LARRY. A tradition? Please. (*To Sidney and Dorothy.*) I suppose you're getting the traditional salary as well, just like the rest of us? That hasn't changed in years either, has it? "You leave me no choice but to raise your wages." Right.

KEVIN. You have no idea how inappropriate that remark is.

ZORAH. Kevin—

KEVIN. What do you think our financial situation is right now, Larry?

ZORAH. This is not the time ...

KEVIN. Let me contextualize this for you, Larry.

LARRY. Please.

ZORAH. Not now ...

KEVIN. We're broke.

LARRY. Of course we're broke. We're an arts organization.

KEVIN. No I mean *broke*. As in "penniless." "Destitute." "Bankrupt."

(ALL are shocked.)

KEVIN. We have a negative position and it could get more negative. We may have to close our doors and we may owe a lot of money.

(General alarm.)

KEVIN. And who will be responsible for those bills?
ZORAH. What are you doing, Kevin?
KEVIN. Who?
SIDNEY. (*Pointing at Kevin.*) You?
LARRY. Wrong.
LARRY. The Board.
KEVIN. No. The founding members of this company.
LARRY. What?
KEVIN. You heard me. (*Pulls out document.*) You all signed the document with Zorah.
PHIL. That was thirteen years ago. Nobody took that seriously.
KEVIN. Well somebody's going to take it seriously. And maybe sooner than you think.
PHIL. Let me see that.
KEVIN. It's a copy. Keep it. Anybody else want a copy?
LARRY. Not true. It'll never happen. Come on. We know how to beat this. We know what to do. A fund raiser. We do a fund raiser.

KEVIN. (*Exploding.*) *This* is the fund raiser! You are *in* the fund raiser! And at the end of this fund raiser *you* say, "You leave me no choice but to raise your wages." And everyone goes home. Happy and resolved.

(A pause)

LARRY. What about the turkey?
KEVIN. The turkey stays.
PHIL. (*Looking at document.*) That doesn't even look like my signature.

(SIDNEY, DOROTHY, and M.J. gather around.)

WALTER. (*To Luther.*) I guess you're not a founding member, huh?
LUTHER. No. I'd like to be, though.
WALTER. Yeah. I'm kinda glad I missed out on that.
ZORAH. (*Addressing the Company.*) I wish I could take back every word you just said, Kevin Trent Emery. To bring that up at this time I think was just inhumanly cruel. Unfortunately you're right: These are desperate, catastrophic times. But I don't want to be too negative about it. I'm an emotional person. You know that.
LUTHER. (*Whispers to Walter.*) She's Lithuanian.
ZORAH. I'm Lithuanian. I have to hold myself in check.
ZORAH. This is a crisis, but we are going to get through it. And we will get through it by giving this city—no, let me correct that: we will give this *country* the best damn *Carol* they have ever seen.

(Applause from SIDNEY.)

M.J. Larry, I think there's been a decision on the cut.

KEVIN. Maybe we should give everybody a break.

M.J. You're right, Kevin. Let's just take a short break to rehearse the play. Places!

(SIDNEY has inadvertently caught Dorothy's purse in his chains and drags it across the floor.)

SIDNEY. Oh, Dorothy, here's your bag.

M.J. Sidney! Sidney! There's something following you.

(WAYNE enters the auditorium at the back and slips into a seat in the back row.)

M.J. *(Getting WAYNE'S attention.)* Excuse me. We're working now.

WAYNE. *(Waves and opens his P.C.)* That's o.k. I'm just entering stuff in my journal. You won't bother me.

M.J. *(To Zorah and Kevin.)* Jesus. This guy is trouble. He said he had an appointment with you. *(To Wayne.)* Listen. I'm afraid I'm going to have to ask you to leave.

ZORAH. Is there something I can do for you?

M.J. No, Zorah, honestly ...

WAYNE. I'm here to see Zorah Bloch.

ZORAH. Well, you've found her.

WAYNE. Oh, well. I'm Wayne Wellacre. I'm an actor. I'm doing a regional theatre audition tour and you're one of my stops. I have to leave tomorrow, unless you hire me. I'm on one of those 30-day bus things so I have to audition for you today.

ZORAH. Ok. Soon as I get a minute. (*Heads back to Kevin.*)

M.J. Zorah, can I see you?

WAYNE. Could I just sit up there and write in my journal?

ZORAH. Sure.

(*WAYNE goes back to his seat.*)

M.J. Zorah, you're making a big mistake. This guy is not an actor, believe me.

KEVIN. Zorah ...This could be him.

M.J. Who?

KEVIN. (*To M.J.*) Sh-h-hh!

ZORAH. He says he's an actor.

M.J. Unh-uh. No. Believe me.

ZORAH. Then why would he say he's an actor?

M.J. Why does anybody?

KEVIN. He could be incognito.

ZORAH. Incognito? Don't be absurd. Incognito. (*Pause.*) Do they do that?

KEVIN. Makes sense, doesn't it? How else are you going to tell what a place is really like?

ZORAH. No.

KEVIN. What did he say he was doing?

(*THEY look at Wayne.*)

ZORAH. Writing in his journal.

(*THEY are worried.*)

KEVIN. What do we do?

ZORAH. (*To Kevin.*) Call the union and see if they've got an actor named Wayne Wellacre.

M.J. Well, that guy is not in the union.

KEVIN and ZORAH. Sh-hh-hh!

M.J. Could somebody tell me what this is about?

(*KEVIN takes another look at Wayne, then exits. DOROTHY enters, followed by SIDNEY and LUTHER.*)

DOROTHY. Oh, M.J., could we have a warm-up?

M.J. Dorothy ...

DOROTHY. I know you're pressed, dear, but I'm paid to do the voice work too, you see, so somebody must have felt it was important. And we haven't *done* a warm-up, have we.

(*The ENTIRE COMPANY has assembled. Some are in costume.*)

M.J. Looks like a warm-up.

DOROTHY. (*Reviewing her troops.*) Right. Shake out, everybody. Shake out all the cares of the day. Right. Here we go. Everybody take a lemon. (*There is some hesitation from the GROUP.*) Take a lemon. (*SHE demonstrates, holding an imaginary lemon. The COMPANY, with the exception of WALTER, does likewise.*) There we are. Take a lemon, Walter.

WALTER. What is this? What are we doing?

SIDNEY. You can have mine.

DOROTHY. Sidney!

WALTER. I'm not very good at this kind of stuff.

DOROTHY. (*Sternly.*) Take a lemon.

(WALTER cups his fingers to cradle an imaginary lemon.)

DOROTHY. Very good then. Everybody. Can you feel its volume? Squeeze it a bit. Oh, it's a lovely ripe one. How big is it? Have you got yourself a little juicy one? A big nubbly one?
SIDNEY. That's too big, Walter. You're gonna be sorry.
DOROTHY. Sidney. All right. Here we go. Place your lemon between your buttocks and squeeze. (*THEY do this. Some with more enthusiasm than others.*) Now squeeze your lemon. Relax everything else now. And *squeeze*-2-3-4-5-6-7-8.

(The COMPANY concentrates on the task at hand.)

DOROTHY. Relax everything else now, but don't let go of that lemon. All right. Low rumbly tone in your tummy. Here we go now. Keep squeezing. Relax your tummies.

(A low TONE is heard.)

DOROTHY. And. *UP* goes the tone.

(The TONE begins to rise.)

ALL. Ah-h-h-h-h.
DOROTHY. What's the matter, Luther?
LUTHER. I dropped my lemon.

SIDNEY. Don't pick it up!

DOROTHY. Sidney.

SIDNEY. Get a clean one.

DOROTHY. Sidney. Low tone, everybody. Walter ... where's your lemon?

WALTER. I warmed up at home.

DOROTHY. Tone, please.

(A light HUM from the GROUP.)

KEVIN. *(Enters, stricken. To Zorah as the warm-up continues.)* Zorah. This is the guy.

ZORAH. What did they say?

KEVIN. The union never heard of a Wayne Wellacre.

(THEY look at Wayne.)

ZORAH. Maybe he's not in the union.

M.J. I told you that.

KEVIN. Shut up!

ZORAH. We'll explain this to you later.

DOROTHY. Ah-hh-h-h-h. Keep squeezing, please.

(The GROUP responds with "Ah-h-h-h-h."
M.J. exits backstage.
ZORAH and KEVIN cross to Wayne in the back of the auditorium.)

KEVIN. Excuse us. Mr. Wellacre, we need a little information for the audition. Are you a member of the union?

WAYNE. Yes.

ZORAH. You're sure?

WAYNE. Uh huh. Yes.

KEVIN. Did you just recently join?

WAYNE. No, I've been a member ... oh ... for a long time. (*Pause.*) Is this a problem?

KEVIN and ZORAH. No. No, no. No no no no no no.

KEVIN. No. Not at all.

KEVIN. Well, uh, Zorah's going to be rehearsing. What would you like to do now?

WAYNE. Would you mind if I watch?

ZORAH. Please. Watch.

KEVIN. Yes, watch.

ZORAH. Yes. And I'd like to hear from you about what you see. I'd like a little feedback.

KEVIN. From an outside eye.

ZORAH. Yes, we could use an outside eye. We've been doing this for so many years, this show, and we may have gotten a little ... predictable.

KEVIN. (*Whispers.*) Terribly.

(*ZORAH shoots Kevin a look.*)

WAYNE. Oh. Say. Gee. I'm not really such a hot critic. I'm an actor.

ZORAH. Oh, yes, of course.

DOROTHY. Thank you, everybody.

ZORAH. Come on down and meet the Company.

ZORAH. Everybody! Listen up, everybody! This is Wayne Wellacre. He's an actor from ... (*Turns to Wayne.*)

WAYNE. Washington, D.C.

ZORAH. (*A look to Kevin.*) Washington, D.C. and he's going to be observing us today ...

WAYNE. No. Really.

ZORAH. I thought we could use a fresh eye.

WAYNE. I'm really just an actor.

LARRY. What'd you mean, just an actor? (*To the Company.*) That's what I'm talking about—The actor has no power because he thinks he shouldn't have any power.

ZORAH. This is Larry.

LARRY. Sit down and take a little power, pal.

ZORAH. Larry's our Scrooge.

LARRY. (*To Zorah.*) I got to you, huh?

ZORAH. This is Sidney, our Marley and Fezziwig. Luther, Tiny. And this is Bart who is Caroler, Petitioner, Fred, Young Scrooge, Dick 1 & 2, Peter Cratchit, Topper, and Ignorance. This is Phil, Cratchit. And this is Dorothy Tree-Hapgood who is Mrs. Cratchit and Mrs. Fezziwig.

DOROTHY. And vocal consultant.

ZORAH. And this is Walter E. Parsons who's just joined us in my multi-cultural initiative to play all the ghosts.

M.J. Places! This is real! From the knocker.

(*SIDNEY gets in place behind the knocker.*)

DOROTHY. Phil ... Phil. In that scene with Scrooge, you say "We *were* making merry." You hear that "R"? The English say "wuh." Now you've got a tiny little bird in your mouth and its life depends on you. Don't mash it. Look at me. "Wuh."

PHIL. (*HE goes to back of auditorium where ZORAH is sitting.*) Zorah. Is there a reason the accents have to be so accurate? Do we have to spend all our time thinking about the accents? It's getting in the way of my process. I can't always be thinking about whether there's a dead bird in my mouth.

ZORAH. Good. And music.

PHIL. You know? As long as we all sound the same. (*To Wayne.*) That's the important thing, isn't it? I mean we only have four days to rehearse this sucker.

WAYNE. Is that a short time?

ZORAH. Music, please.

PHIL. Is it what?

ZORAH. Thank you, Phil.

PHIL. Four weeks, my friend. That's normal.

WAYNE. Well I mean, I know of course ...

PHIL. We can't afford to *rehearse* this one. You have to pay the actors when you rehearse. We don't put money *into this*. We just take money out of it.

WAYNE. Oh. (*HE begins typing, then notices that ZORAH and KEVIN are watching him.*) I'm sorry. Is this a problem?

ZORAH and KEVIN. Oh, no. No. No, no.

(*A door has been set center stage. There is a hole, the size of a man's head, just behind the knocker.*)

DOROTHY. Oh, you've got one of those lap jobs. A man had one like that on the tram. It played a little tune when he turned it on.

PHIL. Tram? How long have you been in this country? Thirty years? C'mon, make an effort. Tram.

(*SIDNEY picks up the chains and stands, not quite hidden, behind the door. LARRY approaches the door, hesitantly, as though moving through darkness.*)

M.J. Cue light! (*SHE starts the tape recorder.*)

LARRY. (*Without stopping the action.*) Is there going to be fog?

M.J. Keep going please. This is just a rehearsal. Fog is expensive.

LARRY. (*Continuing the business.*) But there will be fog? Eventually?

ZORAH. Yes.

LARRY. Just checking.

(*SIDNEY's face appears in the hole behind the knocker.*)

LARRY. I saw him.

M.J. (*Shutting off tape recorder.*) What?

LARRY. I saw him.

SIDNEY. (*Speaking from hole.*) Am I too early?

ZORAH. Just a hair.

LARRY. I have to look for my keys first. That way I don't see you.

SIDNEY. I can't see you look for the keys unless I look through the hole.

LARRY. But I see you. I mean everybody sees you get into place.

SIDNEY. Nobody ever sees me, they're looking at you.

LARRY. They're not looking at me yet. I'm not doing anything.

ZORAH. Larry. Nobody sees him.

WAYNE. I saw him.

(*ALL turn to Wayne.*)

LARRY. There. Thank you.

WAYNE. (*To Zorah.*) Is this the kind of thing you mean? I don't know if it's good or bad, but I saw him. I mean. If that's the issue.

ZORAH. Well ...When we're in the actual light for the scene, I don't think ...

(*KEVIN gives her a warning signal.*)

ZORAH. Hold it. Sidney. (*SIDNEY appears in hole.*) Maybe you could get into place a bit more surreptitiously.

LARRY. Thank you.

ZORAH. (*To Wayne.*) You have to sort of imagine that this part of the stage is dark.

WAYNE. Oh, ok.

M.J. Here we go! We're doin' it now. We're just a couple of steps away from an actual line of dialogue. And ... (*SHE turns the tape recorder on.*)

LARRY. (*Approaching as Scrooge.*)
Fog-Fog-Fog-Fog-Fog.
Fog-Fog-Fog-Fog-Fog.
Fog-Fog-Fog-Fog-Fog.

(*SIDNEY appears at door*)

WAYNE. I saw him. I saw him again.

(*M.J. turns off the tape recorder.*)

ZORAH. I think you were probably looking for him that time.

SIDNEY. Was that too early?

M.J. It was perfect, Sidney.
SIDNEY. Thank you.
LARRY. I could cover him.
ZORAH. Come on, no more ideas.

(General objection from the COMPANY.)

LARRY. It's a great idea. Watch, watch this.

(SCROOGE stands directly in front of the knocker.)

LARRY. Come out.

(SIDNEY emerges, covered by LARRY. LARRY reels back in cartoonish horror, revealing SIDNEY.)

LARRY. Jacob Marley!

(Laughter from ZORAH, M.J., PHIL, BART, and DOROTHY.)

SIDNEY. Scroo-o-o-oge.
ZORAH. Oh come on, Larry!
M.J. Time's a'wastin'.
WAYNE. That was good.

(ALL turn to look at Wayne.)

WAYNE. I didn't see him that time. I thought that worked.

(A pause.)

LARRY. Well, sure. That's a legitimate gesture of the period. I'll bet that's how Dickens would have done it. We're talking about 1840 or something, right? They did all this shit. (*HE performs a series of melodramatic gestures.*)

ZORAH. All right, Larry. (*To Wayne.*) He was just kidding around.

WAYNE. Ah.

(*M.J. turns the tape recorder on again.*)

WAYNE. (*Stands and approaches the stage.*) He could do a smaller version of that. You know ... sort of just a little pullback, like. He could come up and ... (*Onstage now, HE stands in front of knocker.*) ... and just sort of ... (*HE leans back awkwardly in horror.*) ... like that.

(*Pause.*)

ZORAH. Well. That's an idea, too.

PHIL. What is going on here? We don't have time for this.

(*M.J. turns the tape recorder off.*)

DOROTHY. We don't, you know.

ZORAH. This isn't your scene, Phil.

PHIL. I know. And I'd like to get to my scene before we open.

LARRY. (*Indicating Wayne.*) Don't be tight ass, Phil. He's seeing this thing with absolutely fresh eyes.

*(WALTER enters in the costume of the Ghost of
Christmas Past, an odd version of a 17th century fop
with glitter in his hair.)*

LUTHER. Whoa! Sca-a-ry!

WALTER. Ok. I don't get this one at all. *(Displaying
costume.)* Why is this a ghost? What does this have to do
with Christmas Past? This is the ghost of Liberace.

LARRY. He's got you there, Zorah.

ZORAH. This is how we do it. It's a cop out, but we
can't do what's in the actual story. Have you read it? It's a
baby, in the book, that appears to him. It's this weird little
baby man. You see? We obviously can't do that.

WAYNE. He could be a baby. He would be a big baby,
but he could be a baby.

LARRY. *(Immediately following.)* That would be
frightening. A giant baby at the foot of his bed. Could be
chilling.

WALTER. *(Immediately following.)* What are you
talking about?

LARRY. It's about neglect.

ZORAH. It's what?

LARRY. It's about neglect of the Third World. The
giant baby is the accumulation of our collective guilt.

WALTER. No. Absolutely not. I'm not playing a Third
World character. Let's get that *straight*. This is supposed to
be non-traditional casting, right?

PHIL. This is madness. Ok, people?

WALTER. I'm not playing some stereotypical big
Third World baby.

PHIL. *(To Zorah.)* Are we still doing this play? Because
either we stop this insanity or I start shaving off these

mutton chops right now. Ok? You can just scratch Cratchit.

(The COMPANY reacts. KEVIN tries to calm everyone.)

ZORAH. Hold it! Could I see the Company in the Green Room, please. This will only take a second, M.J. *(To Wayne.)* We'll be right back out, Wayne. Kevin! Could you ... *(Points to Wayne as COMPANY exits.)*

KEVIN. Oh, sure.

WAYNE. Has this been too much, this feedback?

KEVIN. *(To Wayne.)* They'll be right out. Mr. Wellacre. I'm Kevin Emery, Managing Director. Sorry we didn't get a chance to ... uh ... I'm the guy who tries to keep the place on top of the ... uh ... above the ... uh ... water. So. *(Pause.)* How's Washington this time of year? Cherry blossoms are ... probably not out.

WAYNE. No.

KEVIN. Lot of crime?

WAYNE. Oh, lots of that. Year 'round.

KEVIN. *(Laughs.)* Year 'round. Would you like to take a look at our financial records?

WAYNE. Oh ...

KEVIN. You understand I'm relatively new here.

WAYNE. No, I didn't know that.

KEVIN. I inherited a very large deficit. I'm not trying to pass the buck. I just think you should know. *(Confidentially.)* I'm doing the best I can with a very difficult situation. Off the record now, if you can, I ... uh ... I think Zorah is an extremely talented person, but ... uh ... wait, that's *on* the record, that part, but ... I am their *first* manager. They never had one. Can you believe it?

Zorah did it all! And frankly, when it comes to money, she's a—off the record now—a nitwit.

(The COMPANY returns. THEY are trying very hard to make it seem business as usual.)

KEVIN. (*Whispering to Wayne.*) Come up to my office later on when you want to take a look at the books.

WAYNE. Oh, I bet they're great.

ZORAH. So. So Wayne, we just had a short, kind of intense, meeting and we all agreed that since this is such a big show, it's time for us to add a new company member. And that just might be you.

(The COMPANY agrees, with strained enthusiasm.)

ZORAH. What do you say?

WAYNE. You want me to audition?

ZORAH. I don't think that would be necessary.

SIDNEY. She has excellent instincts.

DOROTHY. She does.

ZORAH. I do. Don't I, Phil?

PHIL. Yeah.

ZORAH. (*To Wayne.*) So you want to join us? What do you say?

WAYNE. What do I say? (*HE thinks a moment.*) You know, you can be going along thinking you're successful, but then what kind of success can it possibly be if you're not going where your body and your soul are telling you to go? You have to follow your bliss. When you follow your bliss, you come to bliss. You have to cross that threshold. Believe me, I know. And yet, I don't know. Because to know is not to know. And not to know is to know...You know? (*Pause.*) I think before we go ahead with this, I should do my audition. You have to know what you're getting.

ZORAH. That's not ...

WAYNE. Please. You deserve this, at least. (*WAYNE performs his audition. Adrenalin pushes him to exceed greatly the awfulness of his previous performance.*)

Now is the winter of our discontent
Made glorious summer by this sun of York;
And all the clouds that loured upon our house
In the deep bosom of the ocean buried.
Now are our brows bound with victorious wreaths,
Our bruised arms hung up for monuments,
Our stern alarums changed to merry meetings,
Our dreadful marches to delightful measures.
Grim-visaged War hath smoothed his wrinkled front,
And now, instead of mounting barbed steeds
To fright the souls of fearful adversaries,
He capers nimbly in a lady's chamber
To the lascivious pleasing of a lute.

(*HE is finished. There is a stunned silence.*)

WALTER. Welcome to the company, buddy. (*WALTER comes forward and shakes Wayne's hand.*)

WAYNE. Thank you, Walter.

(*Sporadic applause.*)

WAYNE. (*Excitedly.*) Thank you! You know, I've been to fifty-three theatres in the last twenty-five days. I don't know if you're the best, but you sure are the nicest.

(*The COMPANY exits. PHIL lingers.*)

ZORAH. (*Approaching Wayne.*) That was ... that was ... *brave*. Those were brave choices!

WAYNE. (*Not quite down from his performance high.*) Thank you. Thank you. You liked it?

ZORAH. It was ... you were ... so completely ... *there!*

WAYNE. Thanks. What role will I be playing?

ZORAH. Well ... we'll get to that. You must be tired after your trip. Why don't you go on up to my office. It's right at the top of the stairs. I've got a couch up there if you want to rest your head a bit.

WAYNE. That is so wonderful.

ZORAH. I'll be up in a while. (*Starts to exit.*)

WAYNE. "Hey, lady. I like the way you move. I just had to tell you that. My engine's been kickin' over hard ever since I laid eyes on you."

ZORAH. I'll be up in a while.

(*ZORAH exits, followed by PHIL.*
WAYNE takes a suppository from the box.)

WAYNE. (*To M.J.*) That is one busy woman. She thought I was completely there. I was trying for that. (*HE unwraps suppository.*) You know, I don't see Richard III as a twisted man. I see him as a man who is trying to untwist. (*HE holds up the suppository.*) May I?

M.J. Please.

(HE pops it in his mouth and reacts to the taste; takes the box and realizes what HE has eaten.)

M.J. *(Into intercom.)* Let's have places!

BLACKOUT

END OF ACT I

ACT II

Scene 1

WAYNE sits and types at his P.C. A printer noisily prints out a page. WAYNE wears the black hooded robe of the Ghost-of-Christmas-Yet-To-Come. It's too big for him. LARRY enters, carrying two cups of tea; HE gives one to WAYNE and takes a newly printed page of script. WAYNE stops typing and looks at Larry. Rock and Roll MUSIC is playing in the booth high on the back wall.

LARRY. Spike! Spike!!

(The MUSIC stops.)

WAYNE. Something like that? I'm not a writer, you know, so this is a little strange.

LARRY. I think you have a feel for it nonetheless.

WAYNE. Maybe it's better than what you're using though, huh?

LARRY. Are you kidding? Have you read our *Christmas Carol*? Your tax return would be more exciting.

WAYNE. *(HE types a little more, encouraged.)* Thanks for the party last night, by the way.

LARRY. Well it wasn't really a party. Just a get-together to say welcome.

WAYNE. It was a nice thing for you to do, nonetheless.

LARRY. Nobody else jumped in with the offer. What the hell. I don't give a shit if my place isn't presentable. What have I got to hide?

WAYNE. Nothing.

LARRY. Exactly.

WAYNE. Did you just move in there?

LARRY. Why?

WAYNE. Is your furniture in storage or something?

LARRY. No.

WAYNE. Oh.

LARRY. That's it, Wayne. That's the way I live.

WAYNE. Where do you sleep?

LARRY. On the floor.

WAYNE. Wow! And you do this ...?

LARRY. On purpose? Of course. You don't live in such an extreme manner by accident, Wayne. I'm after essential human connections. And material things, acquisitions, they just clog up the flow. You attracted by ads in magazines? Cars, furniture, towels, stuff like that?

WAYNE. Well ...

LARRY. Pornography. It's the same as pornography. It's about desire. You become desirous once you're exposed to it. And then your priorities become very self interested. You let a little of it in and you're lost, you can't stop. You've got to cut it off at the root. Give it up. *No acquisitions.*

WAYNE. I see. (*A pause.*) A towel though. You need a towel.

LARRY. Not really. Think about it. You dry off eventually.

WAYNE. That's true. Boy! So you gave everything away?

LARRY. No. My ex-wife took it all. But I immediately got into it.

WAYNE. Oh, I'm sorry.

LARRY. Nothing to be sorry about. It showed me the way.

WAYNE. It must be a relief to come to work so you can sit down.

(M.J. enters with BART and LUTHER and begins setting up. LUTHER exits backstage.)

M.J. Good morning, boys. You're here early.

WAYNE. Larry was helping me with my role.

M.J. Some party, Larry. You should have told us it was bring your own toilet paper. Jesus, what did you do to that woman that she would take the smoke alarms?

LARRY. *(Handing her a few pages of script.)* Could you get this stuff run off?

M.J. What is it?

LARRY. Changes.

M.J. Did Zorah okay them?

LARRY. She said Wayne could make whatever improvements he thought were necessary.

WAYNE. That's not actually what she said ...

LARRY. *(Overlapping.)* Close though ... Close, isn't that right, Bart?

BART. Yeah.

WAYNE. *(Overlapping.)* No. You said ... at the party ... he said he thought the script needed a little "fresh air," I think you said; and then she said ...

LARRY. That you could do it.

WAYNE. (*Overlapping.*) I could do whatever I thought best, she said.

LARRY. And that's what you've done.

WAYNE. (*To M.J.*) Well, not all by myself. I can't write. I mean I can write things down. I just don't have any ideas. But Larry does.

M.J. Yeah. Larry, we open in three days. Be reasonable.

LARRY. Copies please, M.J.

(SHE takes them as WALTER enters dressed as The Ghost of Christmas Present—a kind of green Santa Claus with beard and long wig.)

WALTER. Where is everybody? Is anybody concerned that I haven't been rehearsed in this role?

WAYNE. 'Morning, Walter.

WALTER. Look at me. I look like Big Foot up here. So far, no one's going to know if I'm even in this play.

LARRY. (*Handing WALTER a page of script.*) Here. Look this over.

WALTER. What is this?

LARRY. New words.

WALTER. Oh come on. I just had one day to learn this. (*Tapping his head.*) It's just barely hanging on in here now. You guys have been doing this for years. You can play around with it.

LARRY. Walter. This is gonna be so much easier. Really. Because you're gonna love what Wayne wrote for you.

M.J. (*On the stage.*) Ok, Bart. Gravestone coming up— Ready ... go!

(A gravestone slowly rises out of the stage floor.
WAYNE puts his hood on and points at the stone with his
wooden hand.)

M.J. Ok, Bart.

(Gravestone slowly goes back down.
(WALTER sits on the edge of the stage and reads. WAYNE
approaches him.)

WAYNE. Walter. Hey listen, I hope you're not upset
that I'm Yet-To-Come. That I'm playing Yet-To-Come. I
certainly didn't ask for the role. Zorah said she thought you
wouldn't mind.
WALTER. That's ok.
WAYNE. If you want it back, it's no problem. *(Starts*
to take off robe.)
WALTER. No. Please. I was having a hard time
relating to that role.
WAYNE. Well, if you're sure.
WALTER. I'm sure.
WAYNE. Good. *(Lifting skirts.)* It's a little big for me.
WALTER. You'll grow into it.

(WAYNE goes back to typing. PHIL enters from the
house. HE carries his overcoat and wears a back brace
over his clothes. HE moves with great difficulty.)

WAYNE. Oh, my God! That looks terrible! *(To M.J.)*
He's ... look ... Phil ... *(To Phil.)* Are you ...

PHIL. (*Moving with great difficulty.*) It's not good. It's not at all good. (*At steps as WAYNE tries to assist.*) Let me see if I can make this. Yeah, this is very bad. That's it for carrying Tiny. No way. Too bad. Strong image.

M.J. Very handsome piece of equipment, Phil. Are you aware you have that on backwards? Let me give you a hand. (*SHE adjusts his brace, from front to back.*) Did you have to go to one of those artificial limbs places for this? That one down on Cherry?

(*PHIL is silent. HE goes to a corner and, with great difficulty, sits.*)

M.J. I'll tell ya that's one spooky place. Not a very cozy atmosphere they got going there. 'Course I don't suppose it would be easy to perk up a hospital supply outlet. I'd hate to be the one to make the choice of what you put in the window. And they never have any sales. You notice? Like, you know, "Feet—Buy Two, Get One Free."

LARRY. We're gonna need those copies, M.J.

PHIL. I am in so much pain.

LARRY. (*Handing pages to Phil.*) Here, look this over.

(*SIDNEY and DOROTHY enter. THEY are extremely well turned out.*)

DOROTHY. (*Entering, to M.J.*) You needn't say anything. We know we're keeping very bad time.

SIDNEY. I couldn't find the car. There's snow.

M.J. (*Exiting with script.*) Yes, we know. It's been snowing for months.

DOROTHY. He's covering for me, I'm afraid. I was somewhat undecided about my appearance this morning.

(SIDNEY and DOROTHY look nervously toward Wayne.)

WALTER. *(To Sidney and Dorothy.)* Do you know who I am?
SIDNEY. *(After a pause.)* You're Walter?
DOROTHY. Yes, Walter.
WALTER. I inhabit the nightmare of Ebeneezer Scrooge. I'm The Ghost of Christmas Present. And I don't know my lines. So if we don't start rehearsing this, you're going to have a real nightmare on your hands. I've got new lines here. I don't know the old ones. *(HE sits in the auditorium.)*
LARRY. *(To Sidney and Dorothy as HE exits.)* You've got new stuff, too, folks.

(The PRINTER spews forth text.)

DOROTHY. Ah well. A fresh challenge. 'Morning, Mr. Wellacre.
WAYNE. Oh, Wayne, please.
DOROTHY. Hello, Wayne.
SIDNEY. Good morning, Wayne.

(THEY converge on Wayne.)

SIDNEY. You got here at exactly the wrong moment.
WAYNE. I did?
DOROTHY. You know if you'd been here just one week earlier ...

SIDNEY. Less.

DOROTHY. Less, yes.

SIDNEY. Five days.

DOROTHY. Five days, yes.

SIDNEY. We just finished ...

DOROTHY. Just.

SIDNEY. Our two hander.

DOROTHY. Only ...

(THEY indicate each other.)

SIDNEY. *(In a whisper.)* Just Dorothy and me.

DOROTHY. Shakespeare.

WAYNE. Ah.

DOROTHY. Quite the best thing in the season. Everyone said.

SIDNEY. We call it "Seething Brains"—an evening of Shakespeare's lovers.

WAYNE. Excellent.

DOROTHY. But it's not your usual sort of stuff.

SIDNEY. Not your "music be the food" stuff.

DOROTHY. It was easier you see, because it was just us. *(Confidentially.)* Very professional. We know what works ...

SIDNEY. ... Just the two of us.

DOROTHY. ... Not that the rest of them aren't professional but ... it's confidence, isn't it really, that makes the difference. I'm English, you see. So Shakespeare wrote in my native tongue, you might say.

WAYNE. Oh.

DOROTHY. From Sussex.

WAYNE. Ah.

SIDNEY. I'm from Cleveland.

DOROTHY. Yes, but you'd never know it, would you?

WAYNE. No ...

SIDNEY. Thank you.

DOROTHY. I think you'll love our "Seething Brains."

SIDNEY. (*Chuckling.*) She does ...

DOROTHY. Oh now.

SIDNEY. She does ...

DOROTHY. I do ...

SIDNEY. In *Troilus and what's-her-name.*

DOROTHY. Cressida.

SIDNEY. She does what's-her-name.

DOROTHY. (*Removes a fall from her purse and holds it to the back of her head.*) And I make her very gamin, you know, very coltish. Sort of ... (*SHE flips her head in what must be a coltish manner.*)

SIDNEY. I play Troilus. (*Imitates the manner of a young warrior.*)

DOROTHY. "They say all lovers swear more performance than they are able." (*Flips her head.*) You see ... (*Flips it again.*)

SIDNEY. Gets me hot.

DOROTHY. Sidney and I were thinking we could show it to you before you move on, you know. You could recommend it, if you like it to other theatres.

SIDNEY. Share the wealth.

WAYNE. Well I'm not actually moving on. I'm in the Company now.

DOROTHY. Of course you are.

SIDNEY. We could just do selected bits.

WAYNE. I'm afraid I'm very busy.

DOROTHY. (*Deflated.*) We understand.

SIDNEY. It would only take ...

DOROTHY. Sidney! Mr. Wellacre needs to get on with his assignment, dear.

SIDNEY. Oh. Oh. (*Privately.*) We understand. (*Finger to lips.*)

DOROTHY.   SIDNEY.
You can trust us.   My uncle was a G-Man.

LUTHER. (*Enters, carrying photos.*) Ok. Folks. Here they are. I got 'em. You pick 'em. I got to FAX some guy my resume shot. We got me happy. We got me serious. Which?

WALTER. Happy.

SIDNEY. Happy.

DOROTHY. Happy.

WAYNE. Happy.

LUTHER. It's unanimous. That's what my manager said, too.

PHIL. You have a manager?

LUTHER. Sure.

PHIL. I don't believe it! A 12-year-old with a manager! What do you pay him? Ten percent of your lunch money?

WALTER. What is it with you? You can't pick on somebody your own size?

PHIL. Let's keep it loose, m'man. The kid's a friend of mine. A status you have not as yet achieved, m'man.

WALTER. And I've been working so hard at it.

(*LARRY enters with M.J.*)

LARRY. (*Distributing the copies.*) Ok. Look this over quickly, folks. Save the questions for later.

WALTER. No, you don't mean this? More?

LARRY. Give it a chance.

WALTER. Give *me* a chance.

LARRY. Phil, is that making sense to you?

PHIL. Shouldn't Zorah be here for this? (*HE reads.*)

LARRY. Wayne, this is better. But I think we're still pulling our punches about Tiny Tim's sexuality.

WAYNE. Oh. Ok.

LARRY. Because it's emerging. How could it not be.

(*General consternation.*)

LARRY. What? You think Tiny Tim never had a wet dream?

SIDNEY. Oh, I don't think that's necessary.

DOROTHY. Really, Larry, I don't think they even have wet dreams in England, dear. Certainly not in the 19th century.

SIDNEY. I think they're more recent, aren't they?

M.J. I know what you're doing, Larry. We all do. But we didn't take your things. Marci did. Punish Marci.

LARRY. Can we do this please?

DOROTHY. What about Zorah? We can't do this without her.

M.J. She got tied up. She's on her way.

LARRY. All right, folks, the moves stay the same; we're just changing a few words.

M.J. Bart, give me a hand with this.

(*M.J. and BART set the stage for Cratchit's parlor.*)

PHIL. (*To Wayne.*) You enjoy yourself last night?

WAYNE. Yes, thank you.

PHIL. You were real helpful about the accents.

WAYNE. Oh good.

PHIL. Zorah's a lovely woman, don't you think.

WAYNE. Very. Very.

PHIL. I noticed she had her eye on you last night.

WAYNE. Oh, yes. I noticed that, too.

PHIL. Did you.

WAYNE. Yeah. Wherever I was, I'd turn around and there she'd be. Sort of staring and smiling. At me.

PHIL. Uh-huh. You know that she and I are ... ah ... a thing.

WAYNE. A thing?

PHIL. Oh, heavy.

WAYNE. Ah.

PHIL. Yeah and we play these stupid sick games with one another like what she was doing with you last night right there in front of me. Trying to inflame me.

WAYNE. Oh, yeah.

PHIL. Don't let her take it any further. Can I ask you that? Please. She's just trying to get to me.

WALTER. (*To Phil.*) Are we doing this?

PHIL. We are. (*To Wayne.*) You promise?

WAYNE. Ok.

(*We are in the Cratchit parlor. BART as Peter, M.J. as Martha sit on the settee. DOROTHY as Mrs. Cratchit sits between them. Though M.J. is in costume, SHE keeps her headset on.*)

M.J. (*Into intercom.*) Spike, get me into Cue Seven. (*To Dorothy.*) "What happened to your precious father."

DOROTHY. (*English accent.*) "What happened to your precious father then? He works so hard. When he gets home—"

PHIL. Wayne.

WAYNE. Yes, Phil.

PHIL. I thought we agreed last night about the accents, Dorothy.

DOROTHY. But that's the way I sound.

PHIL. That's not the way *we* sound.

DOROTHY. Very well. (*In flat American accent.*) "What happened to your precious father then? He works so hard. When he gets home, I'll sit him down beside the fire and ease his mind."

(Offstage LUTHER and PHIL merrily sing a traditional Christmas carol.)

BART. "Tim and Father are coming. Quick! Hide, Martha! We'll play a trick."

(M.J. gets behind couch. CRATCHIT enters, followed by TINY TIM. Phil's back problem has given him a pronounced limp and a twisted stance. DOROTHY rises to greet them. SHE, of course, is also limping from her earlier injury.)

PHIL. "Ok, come on, Tiny. Come on. You can make it. That's it. You are so special. Happy Christmas! (*Dramatic.*) Oh, oh, what's that I smell?"

DOROTHY. (*Flat American accent.*) "What'dya think? It's the plum pudding steaming in the copper."

PHIL. "Where's Martha? Where's our girl?"

DOROTHY. "Well now I'll tell ya. She's not coming, Bobby."

PHIL. "Not coming on Christmas?"

MARTHA. (*Coming out from behind couch.*) "Oh, I can't bear it. I can't bear to tease Father."

DOROTHY. "Let's sit down by the fire, then, Bob."

(*THEY all sit on couch. LUTHER sits on M.J.'s lap.*)

DOROTHY. "How was church, then."

PHIL. "Tiny was good as gold. He's growing stronger every day. Doesn't he seem bigger, Martha, since you saw him last?"

M.J. "Yes, I truly think he'll grow up hearty and strong."

PHIL. "I'm a rich man."

DOROTHY. "No you're not."

PHIL. (*Referring to his script now.*) I am.

DOROTHY. (*Referring to her script.*) "No you're not. You're *poor*. You're poor and you're a coward with two retarded children and a third who's eating you out of house and home." That seems a terribly cruel thing to say, doesn't it? Just a thought. "And a third who's eating you out of house and home."

LUTHER. "God bless us everyone."

(*The CRATCHIT FAMILY freezes in a tableaux.*)

LARRY. "Spirit, tell me ... that boy there—the one with the crutch ... will he live?"

WALTER. (*Reading from his script.*) "He looks pretty indestructible to me. He won't die now. It's too late. But something could have been done earlier."

LARRY. "How do you mean?"

WALTER. "Could Mrs. Cratchit possibly have wanted this child? Did she want to add to the surplus population? Bring another hungry mouth into a family already suffering from malnutrition? I think not. But where could she go for help when no governmental agency will give her advice?" This ... this ...

WAYNE. (*Rushing to front of stage.*) Yes?

WALTER. This ... seems a little preachy. Kind of stiff. You know?

WAYNE. You could do it sitting down.

WALTER. I don't think that would help. This stuff is very hard to say.

LARRY. What would make it easier?

WALTER. Could I do it without the beard?

WAYNE. (*Looking first to Larry.*) Sure.

WALTER. And the wig?

WAYNE. Sure.

WALTER. Great. (*WALTER takes off both.*)

(*ZORAH enters.*)

LUTHER. Here she is.

(*SHE has come from the hair dressers. SHE is transformed from her former work-a-day self into something much more glamorous. Beneath her coat SHE wears a sensual and revealing dress.*)

M.J. Ok! Here she is. Let's get to work now!

DOROTHY. Thank God!

ZORAH. Sorry everybody. My fault. Entirely my fault.

ZORAH. Good. You've started.

WAYNE. Well, Larry said you wouldn't mind.

LARRY. He's doing great stuff. I think our little company has found that writer we're always talking about.

WAYNE. (*A self-conscious chuckle.*) Really. I'm an actor.

LARRY. And you write like an actor. Shakespeare. Moliere. Actor/writers.

WALTER. Can we get on with this?

LARRY. No. Honestly. We know how to *write* words because we have to *say* words. We spend our lives saying shit that somebody wrote who can barely speak out loud in a public situation. And that's their idea of credible speech? (*WAYNE laughs.*) How a person speaks? I'm sorry. Come on.

WAYNE. (*Laughing, holding up* Christmas Carol *script.*) Like this adaptation you've been using. I mean, where did you get this?

(*EVERYONE, even LARRY, is embarrassed by this.*)

WAYNE. My tax return might be more exciting than this.

M.J. Zorah, we can show you what we've been doing here.

WAYNE. I mean, none of my business, but who in God's name *wrote* this stinker, anyway?

ZORAH. I did, Wayne.

WAYNE. Oh.

M.J. Well ... uh ...

LUTHER. It's lunch!

WALTER. That's not for an hour ...

(M.J. signals WALTER to leave.
COMPANY exits.)

PHIL. *(To Zorah.)* Can I get you anything, honey? *(Slight pause.)* Never mind, I know what you like. *(HE goes.)*

WAYNE. I'm speaking out of turn here, actually, because I haven't studied it very carefully.

ZORAH. I'm not a writer. I know that. But it's a way for the institution to make money and so I do it because this place is what I live for. *(SHE takes off her coat.)*

WAYNE. That is so admirable!

ZORAH. I love this institution, Wayne, and I would do anything—give anything—to save it.

WAYNE. I understand. Yes. Now ... Thank you. I have my lunch now.

ZORAH. How are your observations coming?

WAYNE. *(Taking a sack lunch out of his briefcase.)* My observations?

ZORAH. Yes. Your journal.

WAYNE. Oh, oh. I put it to bed. Uh, I put it on hold. For now. Since I have to do this other stuff. But I'll get back to it.

ZORAH. What are your observations so far?

WAYNE. Well, it's really kind of dumb and private.

ZORAH. Well, could we have dinner tonight and talk about it?

WAYNE. Oh, I'd like that, but I have to finish that ...

ZORAH. (*Sitting on Cratchit's settee.*) It's not important. I just need some company. I've been feeling low.

WAYNE. I'm sorry.

ZORAH. I get a little blue around this time of year.

WAYNE. I think that's pretty common. There's a lot of suicides around the holidays they say. People get sad and they don't even know why.

ZORAH. I lost my husband at Christmas ...

WAYNE. Oh. Well, then ... *you* know why then.

ZORAH. He hanged himself.

WAYNE. Oh. I'm sorry. That's ... very ... you must be ... how terrible.

ZORAH. (*Laughing.*) No. Please. Don't. He was a prick ...

WAYNE. Oh.

ZORAH. He was a womanizer. I hated the bastard.

WAYNE. Oh ... (*HE sits with her on settee.*) But you get blue, though. Still.

ZORAH. Well, yeah. I'm alone. I don't miss *him,* per se, but I do miss the, you know, the contact. The physical contact. He was a very successful womanizer. He got my engine kickin' over, but you know what that's like. I don't have to tell you.

WAYNE. (*Moves away.*) So. Your husband. Was he an actor?

ZORAH. He thought he was. But he had no talent. He'd just walk around the stage and smirk.

WAYNE. Oh well.

ZORAH. I put him in this show every year so I could keep an eye on him. He played the ghosts.

WAYNE. Oh. It was probably good casting.

ZORAH. Be better casting now. (*SHE laughs.*)
WAYNE. (*Laughs uproariously.*) Because he's dead.

(*SHE crosses to him.*)

WAYNE. So, your husband was me. He was this?
ZORAH. Yeah. He had an odor that people found very upsetting. And he didn't do anything about it, on purpose, I think, because he was short and he wanted to make an impression. It was so potent. It made me dizzy.
WAYNE. I'm sure.
ZORAH. I miss that. Let's get that engine kickin' over. (*SHE pulls his hood over his head and thrusts her own head inside it, joining him. His hands grasp for the chair next to him.*)
WAYNE. This is lunch. We're on lunch. People will come. Please.

(*PHIL enters and looks on, his suspicions confirmed. After a struggle, WAYNE extricates himself and sees Phil. PHIL exits.*)

WAYNE. I need to prepare for my acting.
ZORAH. Oh, please, let's just ...
WAYNE. For my role.
ZORAH. Oh, come off it.
WAYNE. What?
ZORAH. We know everything. We know you're not in the union.
WAYNE. Oh.
ZORAH. We are doing our best here, Wayne Whoever-You-Are.

WAYNE. What?

ZORAH. Why pick on us? We have never done anything obscene! We have never smeared ourselves with chocolate sauce. We have never shown two boys kissing. I took every last "fuck" out of *Glengarry Glen Ross*. Lasted about five minutes, but it was clean as a whistle. So *why*? (*M.J. appears at the door.*) Why are you doing this to us?

WAYNE. I'm not sure I know what you're talking about.

ZORAH. Stop! Please stop acting!

M.J. Zorah!

ZORAH. You're terrible at this! If you're going to pretend to be somebody else, at least try to bring some degree of conviction to what you're doing.

WAYNE. I've only had one rehearsal.

ZORAH. Well, it wasn't enough. (*To M.J.*) One rehearsal. They think we're that stupid that we'd *buy* this performance? (*To Wayne.*) Go ahead. Do your worst. I don't care anymore. Keep the money.

WAYNE. What money?

ZORAH. You know something? I hope Jesse Helms bites your ass off. Truly. I hope he gets the N.R.A. to bring their little assault rifles over to your building and executes the pack of you. And I hope you all end up in hell where you'll have to watch performance art for eternity. So go back to your cubicle at the National Endowment and tell them Zorah Bloch said to send a real man to inspect her next time. (*SHE exits.*)

M.J. Uh-oh. Cover's blown. Don't you have a cyanide capsule you're supposed to bite now? I could get you one. Well that was enjoyable ... But maybe not thirty thousand dollars' worth.

(A pause.)

WAYNE. Inspect her?

M.J. Yeah. The N.E.A. is probably new to the covert operations game. If they want to infiltrate an acting company, they should try sending an actor.

WAYNE. *(To himself.)* I get it. I get it now. I'm an idiot. So. You didn't want me in the Company after all.

(Sounds offstage of a violent but hushed ARGUMENT. ZORAH and KEVIN enter.)

ZORAH. Wayne. Wayne. Forgive me. I should not have spoken to you like that. I'm Lithuanian

KEVIN. She is.

ZORAH. But I think you should know that thirty thousand dollars is the difference between life and death for us. For me. For all these good people. Please when you write your little observations, don't ... don't mention my outburst. Please.

(A considerable pause.)

WAYNE. Well, we'll see how things go.

BLACKOUT

ACT II
Scene 2
Day 3

The rehearsal has come to a standstill. Everyone is seated:
  WAYNE, DOROTHY, SIDNEY and PHIL in the
  house; LARRY, M.J., WALTER, and BART on stage.

WALTER. I'm not being difficult.

M . J . I think you are.

WALTER. I just don't like mechanical devices under
my feet. It makes me very nervous.

M. J. We start a dress rehearsal in fifteen minutes.
These people have to get into make-up.

WALTER. I'm not being difficult.

M.J. Ok. You're not being difficult. You're being
irrational.

WALTER. I'm not denying that. That doesn't change
the fact that I get dizzy and I want to fall down when I get
close to this thing you've got under the stage here. I didn't
know about this. Nobody told me about this land mine
here.

(ZORAH and KEVIN enter. WAYNE enters from dressing
  room.)

ZORAH. What's the problem?

M.J. Walter doesn't like mechanical devices under his
feet.

ZORAH. We've never had an accident with this. I give
you my solemn oath you are not going to get hurt.

SIDNEY. It's very effective.

DOROTHY. You'll love it when they gasp at it. They do, you know. Every time.

WALTER. (*Relenting somewhat.*) Show me again.

M. J. (*Pointing to a tape mark on the stage floor.*) You stand there. Over the little white mark.

WALTER. (*Crosses to the mark, then backs away.*) *You* do it one more time.

M.J. Walter ... it's ... O.k.

ZORAH. Do it for him, M.J.

M . J . You're standing here. Scrooge says ...

LARRY. "You look tired."

M. J. You say, "My life upon this globe is very short. It ends tonight." You stand over the mark. (*Points to Larry.*) And Scrooge says—

LARRY. "Spirit, there is something beneath your robe. Something strange and terrible. A claw or a foot."

M.J. And I give the cue to Bart.

(*Two FIGURES made of cloth pop up from traps in the floor. They are the ragged children, Ignorance and Poverty.*
SIDNEY and DOROTHY imitate the gasp of the audience.)

M.J. (*Intoning.*) "The boy is Ignorance. The girl is Poverty. Beware of them both and all their kind."

(*A pause.*)

WALTER. No. This has me very worried.

M.J. (*Becoming impatient.*) I don't give the cue until you're over that mark.

WALTER. Yeah, but I don't know if I can see that mark. I assume you don't want me to wear my glasses on stage.

ZORAH. No.

WALTER. Well then we have a problem, you see.

WAYNE. (*It's simple.*) Give him a bigger mark.

ZORAH. There we are. A bigger mark.

DOROTHY. The voice of reason.

M.J. How big?

WAYNE. Big enough for him to see. You notice the man is terrified? Have a little compassion.

LARRY. Right on, Wayne. Speak for the actor.

(During the following, BART brings WAYNE a cup of tea containing a tea bag. WAYNE dips the tea bag and places bag in Bart's hand. BART exits.)

WAYNE. You have to imagine yourself as another person. Imagine someone else's feelings. That's what actors do. We empathize. We know how it would feel for a sensitive person to be forced to stand over a hole filled with puppets.

(WALTER stands back from the mark. The "x" is very large.)

ZORAH. Walter. You can't possibly be that blind.

WALTER. I need all my concentration for my lines.

ZORAH. But everyone can see it out there.

WALTER. Good. Then if I miss it, they can tell me. Wayne. This ok?

WAYNE. If it's good for you.

WALTER. Thank you, M.J.

PHIL. (*In the auditorium, to Sidney and Dorothy but loud enough for Wayne to hear.*) The all powerful government just takes what it wants, doesn't it. It wants our money, it takes it. It wants our freedom, it takes it. It wants our women ... (*HE gestures toward the stage.*)

M.J. Dress rehearsal in fifteen minutes. Luther! Anybody seen Luther?

ZORAH. Wayne, would you like to go over your scene one last time?

DOROTHY. Yes, let's see it. We hear you're marvelous.

WAYNE. Well, it's not exactly the most difficult role in the play. I guess that's why I'm playing it. A character who never says anything.

(*SPIKE brings Wayne a newly painted white hand.*)

ZORAH. But you're finding so many new things in it.

WAYNE. Just walks around and points.

LARRY. You point the way to the future, pal. To a world without acquisitions. You're the most important character in the play next to me.

ZORAH. Your silence is eloquent.

LARRY. (*Walking behind Wayne.*) Silent One, you lead me on.

DOROTHY.   SIDNEY.
Oh, lovely.   Just like Sherman.

LARRY. Though you speak not a word, yet I follow. But this is a graveyard. Is this where we find that wretched man whose name I have yet to learn?

(WAYNE points. SCROOGE sees the gravestone and reacts.)

LARRY. It says—

WAYNE. "That's right. 'Scrooge.' But be careful not to step on any little mice or other creatures of the night who make their home in your gravesite."

LARRY. No. Really, you can't say anything.

WAYNE. This is *my* idea.

LARRY. Yeah but ...

WAYNE. We've *done* your ideas.

LARRY. Yeah, Wayne, but this ghost doesn't talk.

WAYNE. Then I want another role. One that talks. I think my skills are more verbal, Larry.

(LARRY turns to Zorah.)

ZORAH. Well, it's short notice, but Bart's a little overloaded. You could take one of his roles.

PHIL. Wait. Wait. This is unbelievable! I don't care what paper I signed. Throw me in jail.

SIDNEY. Take it easy, Phil.

PHIL. *(To Zorah.)* How low will you sink? You're going to roll right over for this little bureaucrat?

WAYNE. I don't want one of Bart's roles.

ZORAH. Whose role do you want?

(WAYNE, with his wooden hand, points to Phil. PHIL grabs the hand and attempts to beat him with it.)

ZORAH. Stop him. Phil! Don't be crazy!

SIDNEY. All right. That's enough.

(SIDNEY and BART grab Phil and pull him to the ground. KEVIN enters.)

KEVIN. Zorah! Zorah! It crashed! I've lost everybody.

ZORAH. What crashed?

KEVIN. The computer. It crashed with two thousand subscribers on board.

ZORAH. Speak sensibly, Kevin.

KEVIN. I've lost the rest of the subscribers. They were all in the computer. You lost half of 'em and I lost the other half!

ZORAH. What do we do?

KEVIN. Luther. Where's Luther?

BART. I don't think he's here yet.

KEVIN. We gotta find Luther. He'll get 'em back. Luther! Luther!

M.J. *(Entering.)* He won't be coming.

ZORAH. He won't be coming? What are you talking about? This is our last rehearsal.

KEVIN. *(Going toward the exit.)* What's his number?

M.J. No, Kevin. He's gone. He got on a plane an hour ago.

(General alarm.)

WAYNE. He's not doing the show?

M.J. He got a series.

WAYNE. A what?

M.J. He got a T.V. series. He starts shooting tomorrow. His mother says he feels terrible about it but his manager says he can't miss the chance.

(A pause.)

WAYNE. He can do that? He can just go?

DOROTHY. Well that's very unprofessional.

PHIL. Unprofessional? He's a goddamn criminal.

M.J. What, you wouldn't do it?

PHIL. Leave the show the night before opening?

LARRY. It's heartless. We've raised an entire generation of heartless, self-interested people.

PHIL. I want him taken up on charges. That kid will never work again.

ZORAH. What are you people talking about? We don't have a Tiny. We've got an audience tomorrow night.

DOROTHY. Well, we can't do it without a Tiny.

SIDNEY. Maybe he's so tiny you can't see him.

DOROTHY. Sidney!

ZORAH. Who do we know? Think, think! Is there anybody? *(Silence.)* Think!

(THEY think silently. WAYNE rises and contorts his body into the crippled form of Richard the Third. EVERYONE is watching him now.)

WAYNE. *(In the sinister voice of Richard.)* God bless us everyone.

(PHIL attacks Wayne once again.
A redheaded WOMAN has entered at the back. SHE wears a coat and hat and carries a P.C. SHE sits in the last row.)

WOMAN. Excuse me! Sorry to interrupt your rehearsal. Is one of you Zorah Bloch?

ZORAH. Yes, I am.

WOMAN. Well ... I'm Betty Andrews. I'm with the National Endowment. I'm your inspector. (*Laughing.*) Sounds terrible, doesn't it? Sorry. Go on about your business. I'll just sit up here and get my bearings. (*Looking at her watch.*) I've got to be back on a plane at 11 o'clock. This is my only chance to see your work. What show are you doing anyway?

(*ALL stare at her in horror for a long moment.*)

BLACKOUT

ACT II
Scene 3
A few minutes later

NOTE: The scene moves forward as a series of time dissolves, fading in and out on the dress rehearsal of A Christmas Carol.

In the darkness we hear lively Victorian MUSIC, a synthesized orchestra. A pin SPOT picks out BETTY ANDREWS seated in the front row, readying herself for what she assumes will be another tedious trudge through A Christmas Carol. *SPOTS pick out ZORAH and KEVIN, seated together in the back row. The stage remains DARK during the following voice-overs, the*

LIGHTS fading up and down on BETTY, ZORAH, and KEVIN to indicate the passage of time.

CRATCHIT. (*V.O.*) "A Merry Christmas, Uncle! God save you!"

SCROOGE. (*V.O.*) "Bah! Humbug! What's Christmas time to you but a time for paying bills without money, a time for finding yourself a year older and not an hour richer, a time ..."

(Fade out.
(SONG: Any traditional Christmas carol.)
Fade up:)

SCROOGE (*V.O.*) "You'll want all day tomorrow, I suppose?"

CRATCHIT. (*V.O.*) "If quite convenient, sir."

SCROOGE (*V.O.*) "It's not convenient. And it's not fair."

CRATCHIT. (*V.O.*) "It's only once a year."

SCROOGE. (*V.O.*) "A poor excuse for picking a man's pocket every 25th of December."

(Fade out.
(SONG: Repeat same carol from above.
Sound of FOOTSTEPS. The rattle of KEYS.)

MARLEY. (*V.O.*) "Scrooge!"
SCROOGE. (*V.O.*) "Marley!"

(Sound of closing DOOR echoing through a drafty house.

Eerie MUSIC. LIGHTS up on stage. SCROOGE is seated in his chair at home, taking his gruel before the fire.)

SCROOGE. "What's that? Something in the shadows? Humbug. I like the dark. Darkness is cheap." (*HE chuckles.*)

(A chamber BELL is heard. SCROOGE is startled. Other BELLS chime in. They grow to a deafening ROAR. SCROOGE holds his hands over his ears. The BELLS stop suddenly. SCROOGE hesitantly removes his hands from his ears. Silence. Then the sound of CHAINS being dragged. A DOOR, unseen by us, bangs open. LIGHT floods in from a low angle, backlighting the approaching apparition: MARLEY'S GHOST.)

SCROOGE. "What do you want of me?"
MARLEY. "Much!"

(MARLEY gets partway on stage and stops. HE can go no further. His chain is caught on something offstage.)

SCROOGE. "Who are you?"
MARLEY. "Ask me who I *was.*"
SCROOGE. "Who *were* you then?"
MARLEY. (*Tugs at the chain. It won't budge.*) "In life I was ... (*HE tugs.*) ... your partner ... (*HE tugs harder.*) ... Jacob ... (*HE gives a fierce jerk to the chain. The BACK LIGHT whips around and goes out as a lighting instrument scuttles across the stage floor attached to the end on Marley's chain.*) ... Marley! Don't you believe me?"
SCROOGE. "I don't."

(MARLEY crosses the room, the lighting instrument following him wherever he goes. As HE arrives stage right, HE whips around, sending chain and light crashing stage right. The instrument stays firmly attached.)

MARLEY. "Why do you doubt your senses?"

(M.J., at her station stage right, can almost reach the instrument without being seen.)

SCROOGE. "You may be an undigested bit of beef ..."

(M.J., trying to keep out of sight, bends down to pick up the instrument.)

SCROOGE. "... a fragment of an underdone potato."
MARLEY. "Aahh!" *(MARLEY shakes his chains and the instrument moves out of reach.)*
SCROOGE. *(Falling to his knees.)* "Mercy! Dreadful apparition, why do you trouble me?"
MARLEY. "Do you believe in me or not?"
SCROOGE. "I do!"

(MARLEY has kicked the chain back around to give M.J. a second chance. SHE gets a hold of it this time and is attempting to unhook it. We don't see this action, she has it in the wings now, but we hear CLANKING and HAMMERING. The chain is yanked from offstage in an apparent attempt to dislodge the item, making

MARLEY *stagger. We hear the sound of a HACK
SAW.)*

SCROOGE. "But tell me Spirit, why do you walk the
Earth?"

MARLEY. "If man's spirit goes not forth in life, it is
condemned to do so after death. It is doomed to wander
through the world—Oh, woe is me—and witness what it
cannot share, but might have shared on earth. I wear the
chains I forged in life."

*(MARLEY raises a cry and pulls the chain stage left. M.J.
    is pulled with it, knocking over door frame. Door frame
    and M.J. end up on stage. MARLEY, unaware of her
    presence, continues as the LIGHTS begin to fade.)*

MARLEY. "I made it link by link and yard by yard. I
girded it on of my own free will."

*(Stage LIGHTS are out.
The INSPECTOR sits looking on with the same
    impassive expression. KEVIN and ZORAH have sunk
    down noticeably in their seats.)
In the DARKNESS we hear:)*

MARLEY. (*V.O.*) "You will be haunted by three
Spirits."

SCROOGE. (*V.O.*) "Is that the hope you mentioned,
Jacob?"

MARLEY. (*V.O.*) "It is."

SCROOGE. (*V.O.*) "I think I'd rather not."

MARLEY. (*V.O.*) "Without their visits you cannot hope to shun the path I tread. Expect the first tomorrow, when the bell tolls one."

(*LIGHTS fade up on SCROOGE in his bed, a curtained four-poster. A church BELL is chiming the quarter hour. SCROOGE, fearful, is listening.*)

SCROOGE. "The apparition told me that the first spirit would visit me at the tolling of the hour. (*Church BELL chime.*) A quarter past. (*Another chime.*) Half past. (*Another.*) A quarter to it! (*One strike of a deep sonorous BELL.*) The hour itself. And nothing else."

(*We hear dimly, what sounds like Mariachi MUSIC. From behind the bed emerges Third World Baby a.k.a. The Ghost of Christmas Past. HE is dressed in a sleeveless Mexican vest, a gaucho's hat and HE wears crossed bandoleros, diapers, and a baby's bonnet. A rifle is slung over his shoulder and he carries a piñata. Clearly Third World Baby has not been terribly well thought out. WALTER seems hesitant and looks slightly ill. HE stands by the bed and looks at Scrooge.*)

SCROOGE. "Are you the Spirit, sir, who's coming was foretold to me?"

(*WALTER says nothing.*)

SCROOGE. "Are you sir? (*Nothing.*) Are you the Spirit sir who ... looks to be ... dressed as one from beyond ... from the Third World? A Baby. From the Third World?"

WALTER. (*Under his breath.*) I'm sorry. I'm sorry.

(*A pause.*)

SCROOGE. "So. Here you are. Keeping me up. (*A pause.*) You look like my past. Though you hold in your hands the piñata of hope for my reclamation, still I see on your cheek the tear of grief for the centuries of oppression and indifference to which I have subjected you and your kind. Comprende?"

(*WALTER is silent.*
LIGHTS fade slowly during the following:)

SCROOGE. "Usted se parece a mi pasado. Aunque usted tiene en sus manos la piñata de la esperanza para mi salvacion, de todas maneras veo en su mejilla una lágrima de dolor por los siglos de opresion e indiferencia a los cuales los he sometido a usted y a sus semejantes."

(*ZORAH and KEVIN look stricken. BETTY slowly turns around to look at them. THEY examine the ceiling. We hear a Christmas carol sung by children.*
LIGHTS fade up. SCROOGE alone in bed. HE is apprehensive. With good reason. The BELL chimes.)

SCROOGE. "A quarter past."

(*Another CHIME.*)

SCROOGE. "Half past."

(WALTER appears at the run and stands by the bed, one half hour early.
Another CHIME.)

SCROOGE. "A quarter to it. (*HE looks at Walter.*) and here you are. (*Pause.*) Who—"

(The deep sonorous BELL sounds but the tape is cut off abruptly.)

SCROOGE. "Who might you be?"

(WALTER, once again, is silent.)

SCROOGE. "I have never seen the like of you before. Who are you?"
WALTER. (*Under his breath.*) I have no idea.
SCROOGE. Jesus. (*Pause.*) "Well let's see. You look like ... Well you look jolly enough ... Wanna go for a walk?"

(LIGHTS fade. In the darkness we hear children singing a traditional Christmas carol.)

CRATCHIT. (*V.O.*) "He has given us plenty of merriment I'm sure, and it would be ungrateful not to drink his health. Here's a glass ready and I say, 'Uncle Scrooge. A Merry Christmas to the old man, whatever he is. He wouldn't take it from me, but may he have it nevertheless. Uncle Scrooge!' "

(An unwilling GROUP repeats the toast.
LIGHTS up on the Cratchit parlor. SCROOGE and THE
SPIRIT stand to one side. MARTHA, PETER and
MRS. CRATCHIT sit on the settee. MRS.
CRATCHIT has added a few touches to her look
including the girlish fall. Her attitude throughout the
scene is altogether "coltish" and "gamin.")

MRS. CRATCHIT. *(Flat American accent.)* "What
happened to your precious father then? He works so hard.
When he gets home I'll sit him down beside the fire and
ease his mind." *(SHE tosses her head, whipping Martha*
with her fall.)

(Commotion offstage.)

PHIL. Shit!
PETER. "Tim and Father are coming. Quick, hide,
Martha. We'll play a trick."

(CRATCHIT, with WAYNE as Tiny Tim on his back,
hurtles across the stage and into the wings. MARTHA
runs for cover behind the settee. PETER sidles away to
the edge of the stage as CRATCHIT and TINY return to
center stage. CRATCHIT, roaring with pain, hurls
TINY to the floor.)

CRATCHIT. "Happy Christmas! Oh! Oh! What's that I
smell?"

MRS. CRATCHIT. "What d'ya think? (*Tosses her head and then, in a voice dripping with innuendo.*) It's the plum pudding steaming in the copper."

CRATCHIT. "Where's Martha? Where's our girl?"

DOROTHY. "Well I'll tell ya. She's not coming, Bobby."

CRATCHIT. "Not coming on Christmas?"

(*Martha's cue but SHE doesn't emerge.*)

CRATCHIT. "You say she's not coming on Christmas?"

TINY. "Martha."

(*Silence, no Martha. The sound of suppressed hysterical LAUGHTER behind the settee.*)

MARTHA. (*Barley audible, behind the settee.*) "Oh I can't bear it. I can't bear to tease Father." (*More laughter.*)

PETER. "It's Martha. She's behind the ... couch. Let's get her, Mother."

TINY. "Martha."

CRATCHIT. "Oh! What a surprise. My darling girl."

DOROTHY. "Let's sit down by the fire, then, Bob."

(*MRS. CRATCHIT and PETER escort MARTHA to the settee. THEY all sit. TINY TIM leaps from the floor onto Martha's knee and perches there, the malevolent Tiny Crookback.*)

DOROTHY. "How was church, then?" (*Elbows MARTHA into silence.*)

CRATCHIT. "Tiny was good as gold. He's growing stronger everyday. Doesn't he seem bigger to you, Martha?"

MARTHA. "Yes." (*SHE breaks up again.*)

CRATCHIT. "I'm a rich man."

DOROTHY. "No, you're not."

TINY. "God bless us everyone!"

CRATCHIT. "I'm a rich man."

TINY. (*Accidentally striking Cratchit's leg with his crutch.*) "God bless us everyone!"

(*The CRATCHIT FAMILY freezes unsteadily in tableau.*)

SCROOGE. (*Hopeful that the Spirit has recovered his speech.*) "Spirit, tell me ... that boy there—the one with the crutch. Will he live? (*WALTER crosses behind couch.*) Yes?... Yes?... Will he? Tell me please. Please tell me *something.*"

(*Silence.*)

SCROOGE. "What's this? What's this that's entered my mind? This can't be *my* thought. This must be yours. Of course, you have the power of thought projection. I'm thinking your thoughts. I'm thinking, could Mrs. Cratchit possibly have wanted this child? But where could she go for help when no governmental agency would come to give her some help ... help ..."

(*M.J., in complete hysterics, runs offstage.*)

TINY. "Martha!"

(The doorway stage left crashes to the floor, revealing M.J. leaning against the wall in hysterical laughter.)

TINY. "God bless us everyone!"

(The LIGHTS fade to black. In the BLACKNESS, we hear:)

SCROOGE. (*V.O.*) "Ghost of The Future, I fear you more than any spectre I have seen. But as I know your purpose is to do me good, and as I hope to live to be another man from what I was, I am prepared to bear your company."

(The BELL tolls. LIGHTS up on WALTER and SCROOGE. WALTER sees the "x" on the trap and stops dead.)

SCROOGE. "You look tired. (*Realizing WALTER is not with him, HE goes to Walter. and pushes him to the "x.*") Your life upon this globe must be very short. It ends tonight! Spirit, there is something beneath your robe. Something strange and terrible. A claw, or a foot."

(BART triggers the mechanism, but WALTER is standing on the trap and will not allow it to open. We hear the PUPPETS thumping beneath the stage.)

SCROOGE. "Perhaps it was nothing. My eyes were playing tricks on me."

(M.J. improvising desperately, slides the turkey under the Spirit's robes.)

SCROOGE. "What is it, Spirit? I was right? There *is* something there now? Let me see."

(WALTER pulls back his robe to reveal the turkey.)

SCROOGE. "You have ... a turkey beneath your robes. What does this mean? Can you explain this to us? Please?"
CHRISTMAS PRESENT. "The white meat is Ignorance. The dark meat is Poverty."

(BLACKOUT. Upstage LIGHTS behind the now fallen scrim reveal PHIL choking Wayne. Eerie MUSIC: a dirge this time. BELLS.
LIGHTS up to reveal SCROOGE standing with the Ghost of Christmas Yet-To-Come: WALTER in the costume fitted to Wayne. There is FOG. It is nowhere near the action.)

SCROOGE. "Where are you leading me, my silent friend? Though you speak not a word, yet I follow. This is a graveyard. Why are we here?"
WALTER. I don't know.
SCROOGE. "Thank you, Silent One. Is this where we find that wretched man who's name I have yet to learn?"

(THE SPIRIT points with a white hand. The hand is upside down. HE turns it right side up. M.J. pulls the rope that is to raise the gravestone out of the stage floor. It's hung up.)

SCROOGE. "You're pointing to something. It is so dark it's difficult to make it out. Hmmmmm. There's nothing here. Maybe we're in the wrong cemetery."

(*Suddenly IGNORANCE and POVERTY pop up, dangerously close to Scrooge. SCROOGE looks offstage to see M.J. pulling frantically on gravestone rope. HE has a solution.*)

SCROOGE. "Oh, yes. Now I see. Oh, you're pointing to a stone hidden beneath the snow, and there's a name on the stone. It says ... (*HE moves forward at the moment M.J. gives a mighty pull and the gravestone flips up to strike him swiftly in the privates.*) Scroo-----ge!"

(*HE sinks to his knees and drapes himself over the gravestone. CHRISTMAS YET-TO-COME continues to point. FADE OUT.*
The INSPECTOR sits stupefied. KEVIN and ZORAH hide behind their seats.
In the DARKNESS we hear:)

SCROOGE. (*V.O.*) "I don't know what day of the month it is. I don't know how long I've been away with the Spirits. I don't know anything. I'm just like a baby. Never mind. I don't care. I'd rather be a baby. Hollo! Whoop! Hollo! What's today?"

BOY. (*V.O.*) "Today? Why it's *Christmas Day!*"

(*The sound of MERRIMENT and the introduction to the Finale* A Merry Wassail To You All. *LIGHTS up on*

THE COMPANY gathered around the wassail bowl. THEY all hold cups. THEY are a desperate bunch by now. Only WAYNE, sitting on a small table, holding the wassail bowl on his lap, seems to be performing at capacity. M.J. is still laughing. LARRY, his injury still fresh, is concentrating on making it to the end of the song. WALTER stands silent and glum. SIDNEY wears Fezziwig's coat but we see his chains underneath and the instrument still follows him. DOROTHY tosses her head. BART stands by the curtain. PHIL supports himself on the table and sings haltingly.)

TINY. (*Singing.*)
It wasn't such a terrible night at that
Take a look around you
    WOMEN. (*Echoing.*)
Take a look around you
    TINY.
It all happened while you sat there
    TINY and WOMEN.
Dreaming
    ALL.
Here's a Merry, Merry, Merry, Merry
Wassail to you all
A Merry, Merry, Merry
Wassail to you all

We'll be coming to your home
Loaded with Christmas cheer
Here we come
Here we come
Here we come
Here we come—

*(With the sound of SPLINTERING WOOD, the entire
stage pulls loose from the rear wall of the theatre and
begins to tip forward until it hits the auditorium floor,
creating a rather severe rake. The table WAYNE is
sitting on is castered and HE begins to roll down the
rake and into the auditorium. PHIL and LARRY,
holding on to the table, cannot stop its progress as it
heads directly for the Inspector. The table tips forward
and the contents of the wassail bowl land in a tidal wave
on the terrified Inspector. SHE faints.)*

BLACKOUT

ACT II

Scene 4

*M.J. runs from backstage carrying a towel. SHE disappears
into the lobby. After a few seconds SHE reemerges,
moving quickly. ZORAH appears behind her at the
lobby door*

ZORAH. *(To M.J.)* And a hair dryer.

(DOROTHY and SIDNEY enter from backstage.)

M.J. Can't we get her back to the dressing room?
ZORAH. You think mixing with the Company would
do her a lot of good right now?
KEVIN. *(Appearing at the lobby door.)* Zorah.

(ZORAH exits)

DOROTHY. *(As M.J passes her.)* Reviving is she?

M.J. I wouldn't go out that way.

SIDNEY. No. Of course. We understand.

KEVIN. *(Entering from the lobby.)* Coffee. Coffee! For Christ's sake!

SIDNEY. Is she all right?

KEVIN. Is anyone making coffee?

DOROTHY. Is there anything we can do?

KEVIN. I don't see how you could possibly do more than you've done.

SIDNEY. You think she's angry?

DOROTHY. The inspector.

SIDNEY. She upset?

KEVIN. Is she upset? She's curled up in a fetal position on the lobby floor. She's in a state of shock. We can only speculate about her feelings but I think we can safely assume that she's not happy.

ZORAH. *(At the lobby door.)* Kevin! Get back here!

(M.J. enters quickly from backstage holding a hair dryer and a red velvet Renaissance gown.)

KEVIN. Coffee! Is this the best you could do?

M.J. It's what we had in stock. It's warm and it should fit her, ok? You wanna quibble? *(To Kevin as SHE crosses to lobby door.)* Listen. You better talk to Walter. *(SHE exits.)*

KEVIN. Why?

DOROTHY. He's feeling misused, I believe.

SIDNEY. He never managed to say any of his lines.

KEVIN. (*Crossing to lobby door.*) You two can help him out. He's a fellow actor.

(*KEVIN exits lobby door, passing M.J. who is on her way back in.*)

DOROTHY. I don't know what *I* can do. I'm the voice person. He never spoke.

(*LARRY enters dressed in street clothes. HE is quiet and contemplative. HE has a towel about his neck. M.J. mops up the wassail.*)

M.J. Hey! Here he is! Those were some nice changes, Larry. When you look at them individually you think "Hmmmm. I have my doubts." But taken all together ... well. I think you made one hell of a splash. (*SHE laughs. Alone.*) Hey! I'm good! I should be writing this thing!

KEVIN. (*In doorway.*) M.J.! Could you help us lace this? (*HE disappears with M.J. into lobby.*)

(*LARRY sits in the auditorium and stares at the stage.*)

SIDNEY. Sorry about that little chain problem, Larry. (*LARRY nods.*) I'm not sure it was noticeable. We have a tendency to magnify the little errors we make into ...

(*WALTER enters.*)

DOROTHY. Good work, Walter.

SIDNEY. Oh. Good. Yes.

(WALTER is staring at Larry.)

DOROTHY. Bit rough in spots. Bit rough for everybody really.

SIDNEY. Everybody goes up. Forgets a line now and then.

DOROTHY. We all do it. We all forget.

SIDNEY. Usually not an entire play but ...

DOROTHY. We'll turn it around on the night.

WALTER. *(Very controlled.)* I didn't forget my lines. I didn't know my lines to begin with. Thanks to you, Larry. You know what I was thinking while I was standing there frozen with fear? I was thinking to myself, "Walter, even in this, the worst moment of your entire life, you can take some comfort: at least you're not a founding member."

(SIDNEY and DOROTHY groan. LARRY continues to stare at the stage. M.J. enters from lobby.)

DOROTHY.	SIDNEY.
How is she?	Is she conscious?

M.J. No, but at least she's breathing regularly now.

(SIDNEY and DOROTHY rise and move toward the lobby.)

DOROTHY. The poor woman.

SIDNEY. *(Overlapping.)* What a terrible ordeal.

M.J. *(Barring their way.)* Honestly. You don't want to go in there.

(PHIL, on Tiny's crutch, supported by BART, enters.)

PHIL. *(To Bart.)* Careful, for Christ sake.

M.J. *(Laughing.)* Oh, good.

PHIL. I need this. I need this. This is not bullshit. I am very badly hurt.

PHIL. Well, Walter. That was disgraceful. I have to say it. Those are the basics, m'man. You have to say the words. Whatever else happens, whatever else is going wrong, you say the words. You let us down, m'man. *(Pause.)* I thought the accents worked, though.

(WALTER pulls Phil from his wheelchair.)

DOROTHY.	SIDNEY.
Oh—	Walter—

WALTER. Don't say "m'man." I'm not your man.

(PHIL pulls free of Walter and runs to the back of the auditorium, his back problem momentarily deserting him.)

PHIL. I have witnesses! These people are my witnesses. *(HE looks to M.J. who points to her back. HE grabs his back suddenly.)* Oooohh! God!

ZORAH. *(Enters from lobby.)* Well. We got her up on the concessions counter. So this is it. This is how it ends. With a bang and a whimper. After a decade of misplaced loyalty.

I've been loyal to all of you. Especially you, Larry. Do you remember what I did for you when you got here from Boston? I loaned you my car, Larry. I let you drive my

Ford Pinto for over a month with no questions asked, and
when you gave it back to me, without so much as a thank
you, there were half-eaten chili dogs stuffed in the glove
compartment. But like an idiot I have stayed loyal.

    Phil.

    PHIL. Yo.

    ZORAH. What have I *not* done for you? Sidney.
Dorothy. I've been loyal to you both. I'm the one who
cared enough to organize the intervention for your
alcoholism, Sidney. You were moved by that I think.

    SIDNEY. I was. Very. Yes.

    DOROTHY. Except that he doesn't drink. He never has.

    ZORAH. I know that now. I didn't know that at the
time. He seemed unhappy. I took a calculated risk.

    DOROTHY. You might have asked me.

    ZORAH. I thought you were in denial.

    DOROTHY. Everyone comes swooping down. We were
terrified.

    SIDNEY. It was just my new teeth.

    ZORAH. Nevertheless. I think you got a lot of love
from a lot of people that day, Sidney. Didn't you?

    SIDNEY. I did. Thank you.

    ZORAH. Thank you. It's a little late for thank you's.
M.J. My husband.

    M.J. Please, Zorah. Don't.

    ZORAH. Are you saying you weren't responsible?

    M.J. This isn't fair.

    ZORAH. Sherman was terrified of public humiliation.
You knew that. You all knew that.

    M.J. I didn't show him the review.

    PHIL. She didn't. I was there.

(SIDNEY and DOROTHY agree.)

ZORAH. You put it on his dressing room table! Did you not?

M.J. He wanted the personals section. The review was on the other side. I had no idea. You can't blame the review. He was unstable. You don't kill yourself over a review.

(General agreement from the GROUP.)

M.J. Who remembers what it even said!

SIDNEY. "As for Sherman Bloch's portrayal of the role of Christmas Past, I can only cry out, 'God help us everyone.' "

(EVERYONE is silent.)

ZORAH. You owe me. All of you. You owe me thirty thousand dollars. At the very least!

KEVIN. *(Sticks his head in the door.)* Zorah! She's up!

(As ZORAH exits, PHIL, DOROTHY, and SIDNEY rise as if to follow. ZORAH turns.)

ZORAH. Don't you come near her. *(SHE exits.)*

(WAYNE enters. HE carries his P.C. and dufflebag. The room goes silent.)

WAYNE. I know this is my fault. I know I destroyed this play and this Company and this theatre. I want you to know that I'm sorry. I was desperate. I was at the end of my bus pass. Nobody wanted me. Until here. So. I'm not a very good actor, am I? People don't usually tell you something like that. You have to figure that out for yourself. But that's the hardest thing of all to do. (*Pause.*) Well, I'll be going now. (*Various "goodbye" responses from the GROUP. WAYNE turns to go, then turns back to the group.*) I know I don't have the right to ask this, but it sure would be helpful if you could tell me, just speak it out plainly: what did you think of my acting? I'm not good, I know that. But did you see anything? A spark? Anything?

(*In the silence that follows we can hear LARRY weeping quietly. Gradually the COMPANY becomes aware of this.*)

M.J. Larry?

SIDNEY. Is that you?

DOROTHY. Oh dear.

SIDNEY. (*Crossing to Larry with a handkerchief.*) Here. This is pretty clean.

WALTER. All right now. C'mon Larry. Nobody died.

DOROTHY. That's just fine dear. Let it come. Let it all come out. It's good for you. Its cathartic.

LARRY. (*Crying softly.*) I want Marci. I want my wife back. I didn't even get a chance to plead my case. I got back from Nicaragua and she was gone. I want my Barca-Lounger! Not everything. Just the Barca-Lounger. And some utensils. And Marci. (*HE weeps.*)

(ZORAH enters. SHE moves slowly, in a state of shock. SHE sits at the remaining edge of the stage.)

DOROTHY. Zorah, it's Larry

SIDNEY. Larry's had a breakthrough.

M.J. She's up. Is she all right? What's the deal?

WAYNE. *(Hesitantly approaching Zorah.)* Would you let me talk to her? Maybe if I told her it was my fault she'd understand.

SIDNEY. Good idea.

DOROTHY. He could of course.

PHIL. It's the least he can do.

WAYNE. Zorah? Can I talk to her?

ZORAH. There's no need. She loved it. She said it was the first time in years that she'd felt something in a theatre. She's going to recommend a larger grant. Wayne, she was particularly impressed by your performance. You were—I think I have this right—the twisted frame of European male culture trying to untwist. She's staying an extra day so she can see it again.

(A pause.)

DOROTHY. We have to do it again?

WAYNE. She understood the untwisting?

PHIL. Did she mention me?

ZORAH. She liked your anger. She thought it fit your family's disfunctionality.

LARRY. She got it. You know how seldom that happens?

PHIL. I've been working on that. Bringing some of my own anger into my process. It's paying off, huh? Good. Good.

(A pause.)

DOROTHY. We have to do it again.

ZORAH. You have to look deeper. That's the lesson here. Somebody once said that every revolutionary work of art, when seen for the first time, appears ugly to the beholder. And this tonight was the ugliest I've ever seen. But you have to look deeper. *I* couldn't do that tonight, but it is so moving and, ultimately, so reassuring to know that, even though *we* may not see beneath the ugliness, our government can.

You were right, Larry. All along. Thank you, Wayne. We crossed the threshold, but you had to give us that big, loving push. Thank you. Thank you.

(LARRY weeps.

The lobby door suddenly swings open, admitting BETTY ANDREWS. The room goes immediately quiet except for the squeal of Heavy Metal rock coming from the stage manager's booth.

BETTY is dressed in the renaissance costume provided earlier by M.J. With her red hair she resembles Queen Elizabeth I. KEVIN picks up her train to help her through the door. SHE descends the stairs and walks onto the stage, a dreamlike vision of patronage in all its splendor. The COMPANY rises as one.

*WAYNE crossing slowly to her, kneels and kisses the hem
of her dress SHE raises her arms to the Company.
THEY bow.)*

FINIS

COSTUME PLOT

M.J. McMann

I:1 black tights, yellow sweater, orange print skirt, maroon/tan print dress, maroon/grey sweater vest, maroon/grey socks, brown high lace up shoes, maroon/black stripe scarf, watch, gold drop earrings

II:1 black tights, red/black/tan plaid blouse, brown skirt, black vest, maroon/gold varsity jacket, black velvet cap, green scarf, mittens, rehearsal petticoat

II:2 gold tights, green dress, Maroon/grey zig-zag print jumper, green tie, pearls, tie bar, green brocade dress, knee pads

III:1 blue "Cratchet" dress, tan leather fingerless gloves, headband with side curls.

Zorah Bloch

I:1 rust turtleneck, pink sweater, black knit pants, black pantyhose, cordovan boots, red striped scarf, green copper earrings, gold bracelet, gold rings.

II:1 black bra, red dress, black high heel shoes with ankle strap, black wool coat, red chiffon scarf with gold necklace attached, gold hoop earrings, gold bracelet, wig.

II:2 maroon pants, black/blue sweater, cordovan boots, rust/black chiffon scarf, dangle earrings, silver bracelet, hanky.

Dorothy Tree-Hapgood/
Mrs. Cratchet

I:1 coral/grey houndstooth pants, peach sweater, teal cardigan, panty hose, brown Capezio t-strap shoes, heavy sock over right shoe, peach scarf, khaki raincoat, yellow scarf, brown fedora hat

II:1 Tan silk blouse, 2 piece green check suit, half slip, brown mink coat, green scarf, brown shoulder bag,

pearls, fall (hair piece) in purse, rehearsal petticoat, Cratchet lace headband
II:2 Cratchet—green dress, fall attached and pinned up, headband
II:3 fall down, remove headband
II:4 purple/green kimono, shower cap, towel, pink clip

Inspector Betty Andrews
II:3 grey/taupe print blouse, navy plaid jacket, navy skirt, pantyhose, tan boots, olive wool coat, silver necklace, red frame reading glasses, watch pearl drop earrings, olive print scarf.
II:4 red Elizabethan dress, bum roll, white with gold ruff, black pump shoes, hanky.

Sidney Carlton
Marley/Fezziweg
I:1 tattersall shirt, brown pants, maroon sweater vest, tweed jacket, black socks, black shoes, suede car coat, black galoshes, blue tie, grey/black/red muffler, tweed cap

II:1 blue/white shirt, 2 piece olive suit, brown suede vest, maroon print tie, fur collar coat, black/tan plaid muffler, brown toupee, brown fedora
Marley—grey crinoline vest, shirt and pants, grey handwarmers, grey boots
Fezziwig—green coat with vest attached, white jabot with red cravat

II:2 add to Marley—grey crinoline coat, grey wig, head scarf, chains

II:3 add to Fezziwig—white wig

II:4 Marley pants and boots, blue plaid bathrobe, toupee, handkerchief, towel.

Walter E. Parsons/Ghosts
I:1 purple thigh-highs (underdress), black pants, yellow print socks, black slip-on shoes, gold shirt, green cardigan, glasses, belt, bolo tie, black Xmas yet to come robe
Xmas past—silver breeches, gold brocade coat, green diamond coat, jabot, grey/purple shoes, white wig
II:1 t-shirt, green pants, black socks, black shoes
Xmas present - green robe, brown wig with wreath, brown beard
II:2 diaper, huaraches, green plaid bathrobe

II:3 diaper, huaraches, serape', baby bonnet, mustache Xmas present Wayne size black robe
II:4 black window frame shirt, green pants, black cardigan, black shoes, yellow print socks

Phil Hewlitt
I:1 blue t-shirt, canvas pants, brown cord shirt, black socks, hiking boots, brown beret, vest and jacket (carried)
II:1 same as I:1 except rust sweatshirt, back brace Cratchet - green overcoat, top hat
II:2 Cratchet—brown plaid vest, blue pants, black shoes, off white shirt.
II:3 add to Cratchet—tailcoat, plaid tie, glasses

II:4 Cratchet pants and shoes, gold shirt, brown bathrobe

Larry Vauxhall/ Scrooge
I:1 dirty white t-shirt, gold sweater, navy sweatpants, black socks, tan Birkenstocks, tan safari jacket

Scrooge—coat, top hat

II:2 sweatpants, Scrooge nightgown, eyebrows

II:3 add Scrooge wig, robe, gloves

II:4 plaid bathrobe, towel

Luther Beatty/Tiny Tim

I:1 dark green pants, black collar sweater, white crew socks, Nike hightop tennis shoes, red jacket, brown belt, Fair Isle mittens, flue tweed muffler, blue tweed stocking cap
II:1 rugby shirt, same pants, socks shoes, coat, etc
Tiny Tim—tan shirt, brown short pants, tan knee socks, black work boots, tan vest, red Melton coat, green and maroon tweed cap

Kevin Emery
I:1 brown tattersall shirt, brown corduroy pants, brown and blue sweater vest, blue socks, brown loafers, blue/gold/maroon tie, watch, belt
II:1 grey shirt, maroon and gold tie, 2 piece charcoal suit, brown dress shoes
II:2 add green tie, blue sweater vest

Wayne Wellacre
I:1 tan stripe shirt, grey pants, brown v-neck sweater, green corduroy jacket, brown down vest, black socks, cordovan oxfords, black galoshes, brown/blue tie, maroon/black muffler, tweed hat

II:1 black turtleneck, same pants and shoes Xmas yet-to-come robe (Walter size)

II:2 Wayne size robe

II:3 Tiny Tim shirt, pants, boots, coat, vest, cap

II:4 same as I:1

Bart Frances/Peter
I:1 black/olive stripe t-shirt, black jeans, black/olive shirt
  (tied around waist), black leather motorcycle jacket, grey
  socks, black work boots, black bandanna headband, black
  cord necklace, cross earring, black belt with studs, silver
  rings
II:1 black leggings, green cut off shorts, yellow/black plaid
  shirt, same boots, green headband, leather jacket, navy
  baseball cap   Peter jacket

II:2 Peter—white shirt, black wool pants, suspenders,
  black shoes, brown tweed vest, black socks
II:3 add to Peter - coat, green/blue plaid taffeta cravat
II:4 black jeans, black t-shirt, yellow/black shirt, gray
  socks, boots, black bandanna, leather jacket

PROPERTY PLOT

Stage manager's table
Elbow lamp
P.C.P.
Cushion for stage manager's table
Barrel with sign
Pencil cup w/pencils
Boombox w/headphones
Stopwatch
Spike tape
Laptop personal computer with printer
Theatre brochure
Jar of Hershey's kisses
Tiny Tim crutch
White wooden hand
Rehearsal chains
Computer manual
Papier mache turkey
Founding member documents
Managing director folder
3 Christmas Carol scripts
Stage Manager's book
Music stand
Datebook
Bottle of mineral water
Baggie of carrot sticks
N.E.A. letter
Toothpaste and toothbrush
Waste paper basket
Pitchpipe
Tissue box
Grease pencil & checksheet
Christmas catalogues
Swiss army knife w/belt case

Game Boy
Splint w/sweat sock
Stage manager's tool belt
Bag for Dorothy
Crust of pizza on a paper plate
Settee-Cratchet parlor
Script changes
Xeroxes of script changes
Luther's resume shots
Makeshift cart à la Porgy & Bess
Black wooden hand
Ignorance/Poverty puppet
Backstage headset
Second set of script changes
Sack lunch w/sandwich
3 "to-go" cups of coffee
Laptop P.C. case
Financial records of theatre
White spike tape
Pink message slip
Prop food, etc.
Breakaway crutch
Scrooge bed
Gravestone
Cratchet table
Easy chair
Flotsam in keystone
Stage Manager's headset w/box and cord
Lighting instrument
Rifle
Piñata
Bowl of wassail
Wassail cups
Wheelchair
Chains w/pipe

Hammer
Crash box
Towel
Hair dryer
Coverlet for bed

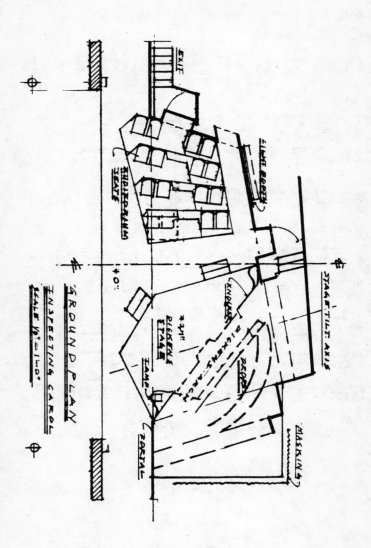

GROUND PLAN

INSPECTING CAROL

SCALE ½" = 1'0"

EXIT

AUDITORIUM SEATS

LIME SCREEN

DICKENS STAGE

LAMP

PORTAL

STAGE TILT AXIS

DICKENS (ENTRANCE)

FLOOR

MASKING

0"

12/91
Lyrics: D. Sullivan
Music: N. Durkee

Merry Wassail

Other Publications for Your Interest

THE BEST CHRISTMAS PAGEANT EVER
(ALL GROUPS—CHRISTMAS COMEDY)
By BARBARA ROBINSON

4 men, 6 women, 8 boys, 9 girls—2 Interiors

Looking for an alternative this Christmas to the old, traditional, Joseph-Mary-and-the-Three Wise-Men Christmas play? Look no further: here is *The Best Christmas Pageant Ever!* The hilarious story concerns the efforts of a woman and her husband to put on the annual church Christmas pageant despite having to cast the Herdman kids—probably the meanest, nastiest, most inventively awful kids in the history of the world. You won't believe the mayhem—and the fun—when the Herdmans meet the Christmas story in a head-on collision! "An American classic."—McCall's Magazine. "One of the best Christmas stories ever—and certainly one of the funniest."—Seattle Times. A recent sell-out hit in Seattle, this delightful comedy is ideal for all groups. It is adapted from the only story ever to run twice in McCall's Magazine, and Avon has over 800,000 copies of the original story in print.   (#248)

A CHRISTMAS CAROL
(CHRISTMAS PLAY)
By MICHAEL PALLER

5 men, 2 women, 3 children—Composite set

Adapted by Michael Paller from Charles Dickens' story. A fresh approach to the classic tale while still faithfully preserving Dickens' magic. At Dickens' home, Christmas Eve 1843, his family and friends ask him to tell them a story but he refuses. It's Christmas—after all—and you can't expect a man to work on Christmas eve. No—he has a different idea. If there's going to be a story—let them each take a part in its telling. And so the story of Scrooge, Marley, the Cratchits and all unfolds. The cast of ten plays over forty parts. "Done with both respect and ingenuity. Deserves to be seen."—Cleveland Press. "A treat. A play-within-a-play that works wonderfully. Could become an annual holiday piece for the whole family to enjoy."—Cleveland Sun Press.   (#5100)

THE BABY DANCE
Little Theatre-Drama
by Jane Anderson

3m., 2f. 2 Ints. Stephanie Zimbalist starred in the original production of this brilliant, moving new drama, both at the Pasadena Playhouse and at the Long Wharf Theatre. She played a woman from Los Angeles named Rachel who has everything she wants in life—except a child. Rachel has located a poor couple who have more children than they can afford to keep, and have agreed to let their latest, when it is born, be adopted by Rachel and her husband. Desperate for a healthy baby, Rachel is paying for all of the poor woman's pre-natal care and hospital expenses. When she arrives for a visit at the trailer park where Al and Wanda live, she is appalled to find that Wanda is not eating correctly. She is also appalled by Al, who actually comes on to her when he is not seething with resentment. The whole arrangement nearly falls through, but by the second act, both couples are back on track. Until, that is, it is learned that the newborn baby may—just may—have suffered some brain damage in the difficult birth, causing Wanda's husband to back away from the deal, much to Rachel's chagrin. Rachel wants the baby anyway, wants to take the chance. In the end, the childless couple do renege on the deal, leaving Wanda and Al with yet another mouth to feed. "The best play produced this season at the Long Wharf Theatre and the first in several seasons to touch the heart so profoundly."—New Haven Advocate. "*The Baby Dance* is not just a 'woman's play.' It is a gripping drama that leaves the audience with more empathy for these people than they would have thought possible."—Bridgeport Post. "A powerful, deeply wrenching drama."—Berkshire Eagle. "It would take a heart of stone to be unmoved by Jane Anderson's *The Baby Dance*.".   (#4305)

THE BATTLE OF SHALLOWFORD
Little Theatre-Comedy
by Ed Simpson

8m., 1f. Int. On a quiet Sunday night, the local regulars have gathered at Burton Mock's general store, in the small town of Shallowford, NC. It is October, 1938. The rest of the world is poised on the brink of war, but the locals aren't much worried about events in the world at large. They're more interested in the local gossip—and Burton's general store is the best place to hear it. The regulars include the gossipy, whining Clunette; fey church choirmaster Fred; lowlife, wild-eyed Newsome Jarvis, on hand with his "slow" son, Doodad; Mr. Roy, a one-armed World War I veteran who holds court at the store; egotistic local football hero Dewey Sowers; Burton's restless young daughter, Ruthie; and her schoolmate Lonny Hutchins, a sci-fi aficionado. All is calm; until, that is, they turn on the radio and learn that the Martians have invaded! Of course, it is the famous Orson Welles broadcast they are listening to—but they fall for it hook, line and shotgun, and run out to do battle against the fearsome threat from the invading Martians. Only Lonny suspects that something is fishy, but he's got his hands full if he thinks he's gonna deter the local yokels from their moment of glory. This delightful new comedy has had several successful productions nation-wide, and is finally available to y'all. Read it if you want a good laugh; produce it if that's how you like your audience to respond. "A theatrical gem."—Asheville Citizen-Times. "Tickle their funny bones, warm their hearts, don't insult their intelligence ... Ed Simpson's *The Battle of Shallowford* hits that magic trio."—Knoxville News-Sentinel. "A sentimental comedy that's hilariously on target. It could easily become a community theatre staple in much the way the works of Larry Shue have."—Knoxville Journal. A cassette tape of excerpts from the Mercury Theatre's radio broadcast of "The War of the Worlds" called for in the text of the play is available for $10, plus postage.   (#4315)

NEW COMEDIES FROM SAMUEL FRENCH, INC.

MAIDS OF HONOR. (Little Theatre.) Comedy. Joan Casademont. 3m., 4f. Comb Int./Ext. Elizabeth McGovern, Laila Robins and Kyra Sedgwick starred in this warm, wacky comedy at Off-Broadway's famed WPA Theatre. Monica Bowlin, a local TV talk-show host, is getting married. Her two sisters, Isabelle and Annie, are intent on talking her out of it. It seems that Mr. Wonderful, the groom-to-be, is about to be indicted for insider trading, a little secret he has failed to share with his fiancee, Monica. She has a secret she has kept herself, too—she's pregnant, possibly not by her groom-to-be! All this is uncovered by delightfully kookie Isabelle, who aspires to be an investigative reporter. She'd also like to get Monica to realize that she is marrying the wrong man, for the wrong reason. She should be marrying ex-boyfriend Roger Dowling, who has come back to return a diary Monica left behind. And sister Annie should be marrying the caterer for the wedding, old flame Harry Hobson—but for some reason she can't relax enough to see how perfect he is for her. The reason for all three Bowlin women's difficulties with men, the reason why they have always made the wrong choice and failed to see the right one, is that they are the adult children of an alcoholic father and an abused mother, both now passed away, and they cannot allow themselves to love because they themselves feel unlovable. Sound gloomy and depressing? No, indeed. This delightful, wise and warm-hearted new play is loaded with laughs. We would also like to point out to all you actors that the play is also loaded with excellent monologues, at least one of which was recently included in an anthology of monologues from the best new plays.)   **(#14961)**

GROTESQUE LOVESONGS. (Little Theatre.) Comedy. Don Nigro. (Author of *The Curate Shakespeare As You Like It, Seascape with Sharks and Dancer* and other plays). This quirky new comedy about a family in Terre Haute, Indiana, enchanted audiences at NYC's famed WPA Theatre. Two brothers, Pete and John, live with their parents in a big old house with an attached greenhouse. The father, Dan, has a horticulture business. A pretty young woman named Romy is more or less engaged to marry younger brother Johnny as the play begins, and their prospects look quite rosy, for Johnny has just inherited a ton of money from recently-deceased family friend, Mr. Agajanian. Why, wonders Pete, has Agajanian left his entire estate to Johnny? He starts to persistently ask this question to his mother, Louise. Eventually, Louise does admit that, in fact, Mr. Agajanian was Johnny's father. This news stuns Johnny; but he's not *really* staggered until he goes down to the greenhouse and finds Pete and Romy making love. Pete, it seems, has always desperately wanted Romy; but when she chose Johnny instead he married a woman in the circus who turned out to be a con artist, taking him for everything he had and then disappearing. It seems everyone but Johnny is haunted by a traumatic past experience: Louise by her affair with Agajanian; Dan by the memory of his first true love, a Terre Haute whore; Pete by his failed marriage, and Romy by her *two* failed marriages. (One husband she left; the other was run over by a truckload of chickens [He loved cartoons so much, says Romy, that it was only fitting he should die like Wile E. Coyote.]). And, each character but Johnny knows what he wants. Louise and Dan want the contentment of their marriage; Romy wants to bake bread in a big old house—and she wants Pete, who finally admits that he wants her, too. And, finally, Johnny realizes what he wants. He does not want the money, or Agajanian's house. He wants to go to Nashville to make his own way as a singer of sad—yes, grotesque—love songs in the night. NOTE: this play is a treasure-trove of scene and monologue material.)   **(#9925)**